Charles Tregenna

Lascare

A tale

Charles Tregenna

Lascare
A tale

ISBN/EAN: 9783337137120

Printed in Europe, USA, Canada, Australia, Japan

Cover: Foto ©Andreas Hilbeck / pixelio.de

More available books at **www.hansebooks.com**

LASCÁRE.

A TALE.

IN THREE VOLUMES.

VOL. II.

London:
SAMUEL TINSLEY,
10 SOUTHAMPTON STREET, STRAND.

1876.

·LASCARE.

CHAPTER I.

WHEN Tom Prescott started on his ill-fated expedition, all the leading smugglers were on the alert. They were uncertain what turn affairs might take. Some of them watched the positions of the coast-guard, while others went to the neighbouring heights to observe any signal that might be made from the Swift.

It had been usual on all previous occasions, when other places on the mainland failed to offer a safe landing, to resort to the island, but now two men were stationed there to prevent any approach.

The smugglers felt that their security depended on the signal that was to appear on Barton Hill. For more than an hour after the time appointed they waited for the light, and at last had the gratification to see it ascend.

As they watched, they remarked how suddenly the pile became inflamed, and afterwards that there was a blaze of light higher than before. But soon it took the ordinary dimensions, and much earlier than was expected entirely disappeared.

There is every probability that the vicinity of the coast-guard was known to Prescott, and for the purpose of securing the greatest light, he kindled the pile at different places; but the cause of its sudden extinction has been explained.

After the scouts had remained some time at their different posts, and conceived that the signal had had the desired effect, they returned, with the view of meeting old Tom, to Tregarth.

He had not arrived. They imagined that something important had occurred to detain him. They refused to return to their homes until they had received his report, for it frequently happened that their schemes took a different turn from what was expected. Waiting a considerable time, and discussing the nature of the light as it seemed to each of them, they arrived at the conclusion that its appearance was altogether unusual.

The lateness of the hour when they first saw it, the sudden blaze ascending from the top of the pile, its short duration, and instantaneous extinction, engendered a feeling of distrust.

Two of them determined to ascend the hill in the hope of meeting their associate, and, if that should fail, to proceed to the mount from which the signal appeared. Not caring at this time that their journey should be secret, they took lanterns to guide them through the darkness of the night. After going over the highway until they arrived at the fields they supposed Prescott had crossed, they also entered, and coming to the hedge nearest to the declivity sloping towards the sea, they perceived the trail he had left in crossing the fence. They followed on. Something mysterious had occurred; they knew not what. How was it, they asked, that they had not met him on his return? They were alarmed at his non-appearance. Still, on they went, until they arrived at the rugged peak from which the flames ascended. They held their lanterns to the pile. It was only partially burnt. They were going around it before they returned to report their ill success.

"What's this?" cried one, impeded in his course by something on the ground. They both lowered their lanterns, and saw the livid face of old Tom, as if staring at them with fixed, but sightless eyes. They turned in horror from the gaze.

Death is terrible in any form. To see at one moment a human being thinking and feeling, and in the next an inanimate trunk, without sense or thought, is a change to shudder at. But these men saw the comrade they had discoursed with a few hours before in perfect health, now unexpectedly lying before them in a lone place, and in the silent darkness of the night, a blood-stained corpse. It was a horrible appearance. They turned away, and looked at each other in terror and amazement.

For a few minutes they were speechless. After a while, one of them said, "Let's look at poor Tom again."

They turned their lights, and saw the blood, partly congealed, still dripping from his breast.

A ball had entered there, and made short work of human life. Now the half-burnt pile and the sudden extinction of the light were explained.

Their compressed lips and fierce eyes betokened bitter feelings of revenge.

"We kum, Jack," said one, "to look for Tom Prescott, and we'll go back to tell what we've found. No, dan't ee cover his face. He was never afeard to show es face. Tregarth never sent a finer man to say. Let that face tell the hugly tale. Let ut tell the bloody work theise villains ken do in a dark night. He shan't be moved till the broad day, that the people may knaw how loving the coast-guard ken be. If they laive wan stone upon anether in that station, I'll give op Tregarth."

In savage mood they turned away. They left the dead smuggler in the same state they found him, and returned by the nearest road. Little was spoken on their journey; they were occupied with their own feelings.

It was still dark when they arrived, but their friends waited their return. In the room from which they had departed they found the other watchers of the night.

"Where's Tom? Where's Tom?" they anxiously inquired.

The men did not immediately reply. There was a deep scowl in their eyebrows, and their teeth were savagely clenched.

"Sit down, sit down, my men," said the chief speaker, waving his hand towards the seats; "and you shall hear all."

They seated themselves, somewhat perplexed at the meaning of this mysterious mode of explanation.

"We found Tom Prescott—brave ould Tom —pun the top o' Barton Hill, by the side o' a heap of half-burnt vuz."

"Why didn't you bring un along with ee?" cried several voices at once, impatient at this deliberate mode of communication.

"Because he's dead!—dead!" said the savage man, bending his fist and extending his arm. "There's a bloody corpse upon Barton Hill, and Tom Prescott's face is looking to the sky for vengeance."

"Do tell us what has happened?" they cried, in impatience.

"The coast-guard have made short work with poor Tom, and have put a bullet into es breast, that has silenced un for ever."

The whole body rose from their seats as one man. Sorrow, anger, and revenge were mingled in their countenances. If the unhappy cause of this commotion, who at this time was fleeing for refuge, had been within their grasp, it would have been his last hour.

When their surprise had somewhat subsided, they were made acquainted with all the particulars that have been related.

" What shall be done ?" was the inquiry of several.

This was answered by one whose fierceness denoted more than his words expressed.

" Let un alone till daylight; then bring un home pun a stretcher, that the people may know what friends they 've got at the other end of the town."

They immediately prepared to remove him, and at the dawn of day all went, in company with other persons who had heard the news, to the spur of the hill, where they found the old sailor, now lying cold and stiff on the stunted gorse.

Placing him on a stretcher, they brought him to the highway; but before they had gone far down the hill, they were met by the multitude from Tregarth.

It appeared that the dismal tidings had been communicated to them in their beds, and they rose hastily to show their regard for their unfortunate neighbour. Silently he was conveyed on the shoulders of his comrades; and in silence, sorrow, and anger the people followed the bier.

They placed him in his own dwelling while the crowd waited outside, and then, returning to the street, asked if they wished the murderer to be delivered up. The people, before so silent, now cried out, "To the station!" and men, women, and children, with deep and angry murmurings, made their way to the guard-house.

When the Lieutenant had despatched the man who, in the supposed execution of his duty, had shot the smuggler, he waited the arrival of his company, who soon after daylight returned from their different posts. He had heard that Prescott had been found, and that great numbers had gone to accompany his return; and he explained to his men that there was a possibility that the crowd would make their appearance at the station.

He ordered them to barricade the gateway, to load their carbines, and in every manner to be prepared to defend themselves.

The men retired to the guard-room, that no show of apprehension might be made more than was necessary; but when the murmur of

the crowd warned the officer of their approach
he directed the national flag to be hoisted and
the men to stand in line in the court-yard
facing the highway.

As soon as the people appeared, they were
surprised at the preparations made to receive
them; and it was clear that if they made an
attack the Lieutenant was prepared for
defence.

They loudly demanded the murderer of
Tom Prescott. At the first mention of that,
Mr. Collins ascended an eminence that over-
looked the wall, to address them.

"My good people," said he, "I am as sorry for
the sad occurrence that has happened to-night
as you are. The man who felt it his duty to
fire the unlucky shot is miles away, and he will
never trouble Tregarth with his presence again.
I give you my word for this, as an officer
and a gentleman. You may storm this place,
and you may reduce it to ashes, but you will
not do so until you have taken the lives of
those who are bound to defend it. That flag
cannot be sullied by a base surrender, and
many of you must fall dead before it will be
struck. Return to your homes, and allow
yourselves a little time for reflection, and do

not add further bloodshed to the melancholy disaster of last night, which is equally a sorrow to all."

This well-timed expostulation had the desired effect, and, after a little consultation, the crowd gradually melted away. The genial character of Mr. Collins added not a little to this desirable termination. He had always been open and free in his conduct towards the smugglers; and although he discharged his duty with courage and skill, he never sneaked into their secrets, or tempted the informer with a bribe.

Therefore the people listened to him with attention. They knew the man that was wanting to the company, and he had escaped; and they also knew the resolute character of the officer that commanded the fort. They retired dispirited to their homes, and a gloomy day succeeded to the people of Tregarth.

A few days after these proceedings, old Tom Prescott was carried to his grave in the churchyard of Lanwarn; and the whole population, except the aged and the sick, followed his bier.

Thus passed away one who had weathered many a storm and lighted many a signal-fire —a martyr to his fidelity. His disposition

was frank and generous. He charmed youth
with the tales of an adventurous life, and
assisted those of riper years with valuable
advice. His judgment was required for the
height of the mast and the shape of the sail,
and he contributed from his little hoard to the
various fishing speculations of the port. For
long, long after his friendly face was missed
on the quays of Tregarth, and even when
another generation had succeeded, the ancient
dames would drop a tear in relating the adventures of the night when old Tom lighted the
signal-fire on the peak of Barton Hill.

While these unusual proceedings were going
on at Tregarth, the miserable fugitive that
caused them lay concealed in the watch-house
of Penwith. More than a week had elapsed,
and the wretched man dared not show himself.

At length an order arrived from the Board
of Customs, directing the chief officer to send
him to a station in the north of England;
and he was despatched to his destination one
morning before daylight, and thus escaped
the vengeance it was intended to inflict.

Rumours of all these exciting proceedings
were carried into the surrounding country, and
gathered as they went. So many were the

stories, that it was almost impossible to tell what had really occurred. Old Rachel Wadge had heard one story at the grocer's, and another at the baker's. The shopkeepers at Penwith stood at their doors, prepared either to hear something new, or to tell what they had heard; and Miss Treloar ran through the streets, without bonnet or shawl, to tell Lucy that the husband of her friend, the island girl, had been taken at sea by a cutter, and was sent to jail.

This was the crowning point. Lucy trembled, and the tears flowed fast over her beautiful face. She went immediately to Mr. Weston.

"My dear father," said she; "I must go at once to Tregarth. They say that Lascare is sent to prison! The poor child—she is but a child—cannot bear all this."

"Thou shalt go, my love," said Mr. Weston; "and I think if thou were to stay a few days with her, it might be some relief. At the same time, I hear, day after day, so many stories, and so contradictory, that I think thy alarm may be without foundation. At such times as these, the probable is spoken of as certain, and the false mixed with the true. A great deal of idleness is one consequence of this sad event. The tailors' and the shoe-makers' shops are full of newsmongers, and the blacksmith allows the heated iron to cool while he listens to some wonderful tale. Still, enough is certain to call thee to see thy friend, and it would be but Christian charity to go. Poor young thing! I love her simplicity and truthfulness, but she is impulsive and pas-sionate."

"I prefer, my dear father, a little feeling to too much calculation," said Lucy.

"Well, well, my dear, we won't discuss that question now. Her virtues are her own, her failings are the fault of other people."

"I don't think Edith has any failing."

"Was it no failing," said the Quaker, "that she clung to thee with such ungovernable passion, and then flung herself on the beach in such reckless despair?"

"Oh! if her failing be that she loves me too much, I will forgive her. I will go at once; and as the sea is stormy, I will walk to Tregarth, and thinking of her *failing*, will make the journey light."

CHAPTER II.

In the afternoon of the day that the report had been circulated of the capture of Lascare, Lucy Weston took her journey alone to Tregarth. Her father did not keep a carriage—very few Quakers of that day indulged in the luxury— and Lucy's equestrian experience had not proceeded further than some journeys on a pillion. Once she rode alone, and that was on a pannel, when she went with the Kellys to Lanwarn. The side-saddle was a novelty, that had just arrived in the neighbourhood, and it was used by a baronet's daughter. Ladies of the middle class generally walked the short journeys, and they were the better for it.

Lucy took the pathway over the cliffs, and a more lovely walk England cannot produce. Of late the sea-side excursions had become the favourites. She was accustomed to look over the pathless sea, as if there was something far, far away, that was very dear to her. She preferred being alone on those occasions, because she could ponder without interruption, and wander on.

On her journey to Tregarth she thought alternately of George Millett and Edith Lascare, and then again of them both together; for if George were home she would claim his advice and assistance for the liberation of the smuggler. She wished Edith had not married that wild, restless, reckless man; but now those that love Edith must help Lascare. Who could forsake that lonely married girl, bereft of kith and kin, whose greatest failing was that she loved too fondly?

Then her mind recurred again to her own position. " I will obey my dear, kind-hearted father," said she, to herself. " I will never marry without his consent ; but to forget George Millett, as I am expected to do, is beyond my power. Do people think that one's affections can be put off and on, as things suitable or inconvenient ? If I could think him unworthy, base, and insincere, I could forget him ; but then he would not be George Millett."

Musing in this way, she arrived at Tregarth. The sun had gone down, and the short twilight of an autumn evening was disappearing when she came to Edith's cottage.

A stately old dame, with high cap and stiff bodice, and dark chintz dress, was sitting with Edith by the fireside. Her complexion was dark and clear, and her countenance composed. She rose to depart at the entrance of a strange lady; but before Edith allowed her to do so, she introduced Miss Weston to Mrs. Spillar.

" My name is Mary Spillar, if you plaise," said the wife of the ancient mariner.

" And my name," said the Quaker's daughter, smiling, " is Lucy Weston. I am glad to make your acquaintance, for I often hear my father speak of your husband. He entertains a high respect for him."

" I 'm sure, Miss Weston, I 'm very much obloiged to ee for sayin' so. I wish ee good eiveling."

" Good evening, Mrs. Spillar," said Lucy, holding out her hand, and smiling in a very friendly manner. " When you can call me by my proper name, I shall be able to speak yours."

Edith was standing behind them as Mrs. Spillar left, and a smile forced itself on her saddened countenance at their friendly altercation.

" I thank you very, very much for coming," said she.

" Where is your husband ?" asked Lucy.

" At Crosaix."

" Then it is not true that he was taken at sea by a cutter ?"

" No, thank Heaven ! Did you hear that he was ?"

" Yes," said Lucy ; " and that is the cause of my journey."

" It is very kind of you, and for once a false report has done me a good turn. I am happy to say Richard is safe in port, and I have received a letter from him to-day."

It appeared by the letter that the danger signal had been perceived, and all attempt to effect a landing had been postponed. After spending some time in the Channel, and approaching the coast at night-time without any signal of encouragement, they resolved to return to Crosaix, there to refit, and replenish their stores.

Lascare wrote in good spirits, and seemed rather to enjoy the sensation his approach had created; but he was ignorant of its fatal result.

" We sailed," he said in a part of his letter,

" close to the mouth of the harbour, and saw the lights in the windows, but did not dare to land. I was longing to see you. If it was uncle Tom that sent up the flame, he was determined we should see it, for I never saw a better light, although its duration was short. We shall remain here until the stormy weather is over, and then try the coast again. Almost daily there is a man walking to and fro on the quay, casting sidelong glances at the Swift. He is a sour, cut-throat looking fellow. We begin to think we are watched; and that will account for their knowledge of our last voyage."

" That is good news," said Lucy, " so far as it shows that he is safe. How much better he writes than sailors generally."

" Yes," said Edith. " When we sit alone, he relates all the circumstances of his former life. A schoolmistress of the village taught him to read, and, after that, his father placed him under the instruction of a deformed old schoolmaster. The mental acquirements of that man were superior to his station. Perhaps his deformity prevented his rise in the world. However, he was a kind old man, for as Richard's father could not afford more than six months' education, he gave him instruction for six months longer without charge. Altogether it was a very short time, and, of course, he could not learn very much; but it was the foundation on which he improved himself. He is very fond of reading, and he can tell the origin and progress of all the wars. I wish he was not so very fond of that kind of reading, because I think it inspires him with a love of adventure. Tumult and danger seem a pleasure to him. I suppose you have heard of the death of poor Tom Prescott, who was shot by the coast-guard?"

"Yes, I heard of that, and also of the threatened attack on the station."

"The horrors of that dismal week did not end there. It was our misfortune to have a man living in the town who was not appalled by the fatal cloud that was over us. He had determined to try the courage of one of our fishermen, who professed not to fear the spirits of the dead. Joseph Boroughs was returning alone in the dark night from uncle Tom's funeral, when, turning a corner of the road, he suddenly saw the appearance of a person in white—the image of a dead man, clothed in his shroud—standing on the hedge.

" 'In the name of Heaven,' he said, ' what is it ?'

" 'I am—the ghost—of Thomas Prescott,' it answered, in slow and unearthly tones.

"Boroughs trembled in every limb. His whole body was convulsed. His eyes projected from their sockets. He gazed at the image with a horrible fascination, and fell senseless to the ground.

" Some neighbours returning a little later, found him lying across the road. At first he had the appearance of one dead; but the body was warm, and he seemed to breathe. They managed to carry him; but whether it was a stranger, or one of their own town, they did not know. At the first house they came to they called for a light, and then they saw the features of poor Joseph Boroughs."

" But how came it that he was alone, when so many were at the funeral?" asked Lucy.

" They have their funerals in the afternoon, and, at this time of the year, night comes on before they return, Lanwarn Church being three miles off. Other persons, who were in collusion, had placed themselves in company with Boroughs, and left him before they arrived at the place appointed."

"What was the result?"

"Three days after the man died. The shock killed him."

"Did he recover his senses?"

"Yes. On the second day his reason returned. He said that he saw the ghost of Tom Prescott on the hedge, and he felt his hair stand on end. He could not turn his eyes from the sight; but he remembered nothing more."

"How, then, did you know in what manner it occurred?"

"When the man who caused the mischief heard that his victim was dying, struck with remorse, and thinking that his confession might save him, he went to his bed-side, and, asking his forgiveness, said it was he that stood on the hedge. But it was too late; the mischief was done. The day after Boroughs died."

After relating this story, Edith was much affected, and her former dejection, which Lascare's letter had removed, again returned.

"My dear Edith," said Lucy, "I often look on the happy days we spent on the island, and think you must regret the loss of them."

"'Tis very true; those days were happy

ones," said Edith. "But we cannot always be
children. When you and I played on the
sand, and threw pebbles into the sea, we
spent the sunny hours without care for the
future, or regret for the past; but it would be
an unsuitable occupation now. Every age
brings its own pleasure, and its own sorrow;
but the sorrows thicken as time creeps on. I
could have lived contentedly on the island if
Richard had not loved me; but, if I had
refused to marry, who would have taken care
of Richard?"

"I should think," said Lucy, with a spice of
satire in her tone, and speaking in slow and
measured time, "I should think that Richard
was old enough, and big enough, and strong
enough to take care of himself. Besides, I
don't know that it was necessary that you
should sacrifice your happiness to take care of
Richard!"

"My dear Lucy, you don't know him. He
will never be old enough to take care of himself. If it depended on size and strength, you
would certainly be right; but, unfortunately,
danger and opposition urge him on. He is
generous, truthful, and brave; he is noble, but
he is passionate and impetuous; and so reck-

less of consequences that he requires the guidance of a loving hand.

"I will tell you a secret. There was no necessity that he should have gone to the island on the day that threatened to be his last. The next day would have done as well, or the week after. He went in that hurricane for no other object but to see me. He could not well go to the island without some business for an excuse; for I did not know whether I liked him, and he was generally avoided. When he had some scheme to reveal, that had the appearance of an object, no storm deterred him. I saw him in the surf. struggling for life. I alone knew why he had come. I saw the man that loved me intensely hurled towards the shore, and as rapidly swept off by the resistless current. I cared for nothing—I saw no risk—and I saved him! You may think that in some things Richard might be better. I don't want him better. I love him as he is."

"I have no doubt, my dear," said Lucy, "that you have a very good husband, who is a brave and noble man, but when he comes home again you must persuade him to discontinue these hazardous voyages, and you will then live a peaceful and happy life."

Edith smiled with gratification. She wished above all things that Richard should be esteemed, and, above all others in the world, by Lucy Weston.

"There is a gentleman far away across the ocean," she said, "that I feel an interest in. Have you heard from him lately?"

"I have heard of him, but not from him. Mrs. Kelly comes to me after the arrival of every mail, to let me know of his welfare. I am looking forward to his arrival, not to see him, but to know that he is safe in his native land. I must not see him. Not that he would try to persuade me to oppose my father, but seeing him would make obedience more painful."

Lucy Weston spent several days at Tregarth. The excitement of the place was subsiding. Edith was not under any apprehension for her husband, because he was safe at Crosaix; and another letter had arrived through Mr. Drew, the banker — for their correspondence was secretly conducted — announcing that Lascare only waited for a favourable wind.

Edith accompanied Lucy a long distance on her return to Penwith, and after the foster-sisters had parted, Lucy again pondered over her friend's description of Lascare. She had never seen him, but his dexterity in deluding the Government had become famous. He was certainly no ordinary man, nor was it wonderful that the imaginative mind of Edith had been captivated by his roving disposition.

"He is impetuous, bold, and daring," she said to herself, "and—reckless of consequences. Until Edith came to that last characteristic, it seemed as if she was describing George Millett; but George is not reckless. The difference, perhaps, is partly the result of temperament—partly of education. But he too requires the guiding hand; and oh! how I yearn for the right to give it. But it may never be. The period of his service is coming on, and, as the time draws near, I am losing my hope. At this moment, perhaps, he is sailing to these shores. What a priceless life— priceless to me—is on the ocean. But I must school my heart to duty, not to love. If I could marry him without consent, I should bring my father to the grave, and bring to George Millett the misery of a remorseful wife. That must never be!"

CHAPTER III.

SOME weeks after Lucy's visit to Tregarth the ship to which George Millett had been appointed, having fulfilled her mission, returned from her voyage, and in consideration of his services he was promoted to the rank of commander.

Mr. and Mrs. Millett had been for months looking forward to their son's return. They had missed him very much, for the rector was of retiring habits, his time being chiefly occupied in his farm and his books, and the rattling conversation of George was a condiment of great value.

The elder son made his appearance for a week once in the year; but he made no secret of the sacrifice he underwent on those occasions, and said that the whole county was *slow*.

They were sitting down at the breakfast-table on the morning after George's return, and the newly-made captain had to reply to various inquiries relating to the countries he had visited and the people he had seen.

" I am sorry you were not here last week, George," said his father, " because you would have had an opportunity of signing the petition against Catholic emancipation, which I felt it my duty to take around the parish for signatures."

" There is nothing to regret in that case," said his son, " because I am afraid I could not have obliged you."

" Oh ! George," said Mrs. Millett, " I hope you are not a Catholic ? "

" I was never more distant from such a consummation ; but I have seen more people of other creeds since I left, and especially Roman Catholics ; and I have too high a regard for them to do anything that would prevent the attainment of that distinction which their merits deserve."

" But, my dear boy," (the old gentleman still wished to patronize him, as a youth,) " the existence of the Protestant religion is at stake."

" That is what Peel says. We get the newspapers in files, and having plenty of time to read, we take them in order ; and I know the arguments of all. That young man spins out a speech as smooth as his father's yarn, but there is no brilliancy in it."

" Then who are your brilliant men ? "

" On this question," said the captain, " they are certainly not on your side. You have Castlereagh, Percival, Vansittart, and Peel, and a host of others, who would not open their mouths on the subject, if there had been men of mark to support their views.

" On the other side are Canning, Brougham, Grey, Huskisson, Palmerston, Plunkett, and Mackintosh. Where there is such a preponderance of talent, the result is inevitable."

" I am of a different opinion," said the rector. " I am quite alarmed at the rebellion that O'Connell is fomenting. Mr. Shaw says that he threatens to paint death's head and cross-bones over the door-post of every elector who does not vote for emancipation."

" I saw that, sir, in the papers; and also that O'Connell replied that he would paint over the door-post of Recorder Shaw, ' calf's-head and jaw-bones'; and if I was chief herald I would add, as a motto to those armorial bearings, ' *Fuimus*,' that the world might know from what distinguished ancestry he had descended."

" With the parties so evenly divided on the

subject," said Mr. Millett, "I am afraid the Government is in a critical position."

"I wish," said his son, "that the Government were driven from office."

"My dear George," said Mrs. Millett, "your brother John entertains very different opinions."

"No doubt he does. He is in the pet service. Any amount of money can be spent about the army, because they happen to have a royal duke for commander-in-chief; and the navy may go to the dogs. He doesn't believe, I suppose, that Mrs. Clarke sold the commissions? The navy does believe it. While the army is indulged in every whim, the navy is curtailed in every branch, and the officers are snubbed by that offensive Secretary to the Admiralty, Wilson Croker, who is allowed to have more swing than the First Lord himself."

"Where, George, do you get all this information?" asked his father.

"In the ward-room, where there is a great deal of sense, as well as nonsense, on the board."

"Then why didn't you bring home the sense, and leave the nonsense behind?"

" Because, with submission be it spoken, I was my father's son."

"I think you merited that, John," said Mrs. Millett, laughing, who had begun to feel that the navy was neglected.

"Can I have your pony, sir, this morning, to ride over to Tredart?"

"Yes, you can; but don't ride her fast—she is so fat. I thought you would look at my Swede turnips this morning. They are the finest in the parish; and mine was the finest ox in Lezant fair."

"I will look at the turnips and oxen to-morrow. I suppose you are making a fortune with your farm?"

"I get a great deal of *glory*, George, but very little *cash*. I ventured a great deal of corn in my beautiful ox, but, as a speculation, it was a bad investment."

The rector thought his son intended to call at Tredart to inquire for his friends; but Mrs. Millett suspected that there was an ulterior design.

Soon after the conversation alluded to, he rode over to Tredart, and was warmly welcomed by his old friends. He opened his mind without reserve to Mrs. Kelly, and engaged the services of that zealous lady to make known his arrival, and to ask Lucy if he might be allowed to address her father with another application.

If that should be deemed unadvisable, his next request was that he might see her, and, that failing, that he might write to her.

Mrs. Kelly assured George that Lucy felt unabated interest in his welfare, and had been made fully acquainted with all the incidents of his voyage. Mrs. Kelly, herself, was not without hope that Mr. Weston would ultimately relent; but she must faithfully deliver a message from Lucy, which, expecting his return, she had desired her to take the first opportunity to communicate. It was to this effect: that after what had occurred, she had no claim on him; that she could not expect and did not wish that he should abandon all his prospects in life by waiting for her, which might be fruitless at last; and bitter as all severance of hope would be, it could hardly be worse than the painful feelings she suffered from the reflection that their indefinite position towards each other was blasting the fortunes of his otherwise prosperous life.

When Mrs. Kelly had delivered the message

she waited to watch its effect. She scanned the countenanc of the young man, that she might read there the feelings of the heart.

At first he could make no reply; but it was evident that he was harassed by very painful sensations. He turned his head away, but not before she perceived a tear stealing over his manly face. At length he turned to reply, and his countenance denoted fixed resolution.

"Tell her, my dear Mrs. Kelly," said he, "that until she disowns me, until she spurns my love, I will hope for her, and wait for her. Tell her she is the solace of my life, if she can only think kindly of me; that I shall be happy to know she values my love, even if fate should prevent our union. But, Mrs. Kelly," said he, energetically, "nothing will prevent it. We shall live to be united."

We must do Mrs. Kelly the justice to say that her interest in the affairs of Lucy Weston and George Millett proceeded from a generous desire to benefit both. It was by accident that they became acquainted with each other at her house, although their meeting suggested what afterwards occurred.

The hearts of both being unoccupied by any previous attachment—the one a beautiful girl, of an age when the intellect gives a tone to the beauty of youth, the other a fine, handsome fellow, with the frankness of a sailor and the deportment of a gentleman—it was most natural that they should be fascinated with each other's society.

Added to this was the charm of a cultivated mind, and a bewitching pleasantry that enlivened the conversation of one, and the strong common-sense, varied information, and the impetuous stream of original thought that adorned the other.

It is scarcely conceivable that two such persons, placed in the neighbourhood of warbling birds, murmuring streams, and echoing woodlands, could be otherwise than enchanted. Cupid frequents the sunny glade and the grass-grown lane more than the gilded saloon or the flaunting dance.

It is useless for sagacious people to point out the incongruity of such an attachment,—a Quakeress with a Churchman, a tradesman's daughter with a gentleman's son, a child of peace with a son of war. There have always been incongruous attachments, and there always will be; and frequently the most suitable in appearance is in reality the most inappropriate.

These two were not endowed with the calculations that pertain to more advanced age; and sorry should we be to see the experience of senility sway the feelings and depress the aspirations of youth.

There would be less sorrow in the world, we shall be told, with more calculation and a limited sensibility. A very doubtful assertion. There would be hard, cold, calculating, ungenerous souls filling the habitable globe; and the pleasures that make life bearable would be diminished.

Mrs. Kelly did not endeavour to prevent the growing attachment of two persons that she greatly esteemed. On the contrary, feeling that the quiet consideration of Lucy would be a wholesome restraint on the impetuous sailor, she fostered, with the aid of opportunity, an attachment which appeared to her greatly to be desired.

She had not foreseen the difficulties, she thought them most unreasonable; but, unhappily, they were insuperable; and she felt it a duty to soothe the feelings that she had been instrumental in wounding. Both parties had made her the confidante of their sorrows, and she spared no pains to render them assistance.

When, therefore, George Millett expressed his determination to abide the issue, and his confidence that it would be successful at last, she perceived that the long voyage had caused no abatement of his affections, and she determined that nothing should be wanting on her part to effect the union that her two friends so earnestly desired.

The conversation between Mrs. Kelly and Captain Millett—for we must give him the title he had acquired—was now directed to the best mode of obtaining his object.

"Will you kindly ask her if I might be permitted to apply to Mr. Weston again, and beseech him to consent to our engagement? I feel that I could plead my cause with considerable effect, for he might have thought that mine was the wild and fleeting passion of a young man for a pretty girl. Now at least he must know that, not having seen or corresponded with her for three long years, and being still ready to devote my life to her happiness, it is not the weak impression of an unstable man."

"I think there is a great deal in what you say," said Mrs. Kelly; "and I will urge it on

Lucy ; but she herself will be the wisest judge of the proper course."

"I know," said he, "that her keen sense of duty would be pained by adopting any line her father would not approve ; but surely such an unusual adherence to rectitude should of itself have some weight with a kind and indulgent parent. I have no personal knowledge of Mr. Weston, but from the impression I derived from Lucy, as well as from other sources of information, I conceive he is taking the course he considers most conducive to the happiness of his daughter. If we could divest him of that opinion, there would be some hope of a speedy compliance."

"I should be glad," said Mrs. Kelly, "if that was the only obstacle ; but I am afraid that other powerful motives will affect the course of Mr. Weston. He is an important member of his Society, and a strict observer of its rules and practice. It is a fundamental principle that they shall not marry except it be within the pale of their connexion ; and he would conceive that a connivance at any infringement of that regulation would tend to the disorganization of his Church, and undermine the foundation of his own influence."

"I am afraid," said the Captain, "that my profession is also very repugnant to his feelings."

"No doubt about it," said Mrs. Kelly; "and also the profession of your father. The two professions that are held in the greatest detestation by Quakers are those that are destined for the prosecution of war and for the support of the Church. Your position in that respect is most unhappy. Yet I have never seen, in the course of my experience, a reasonable and warm attachment of two honourable and intelligent persons fail of its object."

"Thank you, Mrs. Kelly," said George, warmly. "You don't know the pleasure you give me."

On the morning following this visit to Tredart, the good old parson explained a project he had conceived of making a little capital out of the Captain's late promotion and safe return.

"My dear boy," he began, "you are rather a favourite with the farmers around, and I wish to use your services for the purpose of making a very disagreeable duty as little irksome as possible."

George looked up in astonishment, and

asked,—" In what possible way can I be of
service ? "

" You can make the sight of your father less
hateful."

" My dear father, to do that I will go to
the end of the world with you, though I am
puzzled to understand what can make your
pleasant countenance disagreeable."

" It is the errand that I am going on,
George, that is so unpleasant. There is not
a farmer in the parish that would not entertain
me for a week, if I wished it; and would
spread his table with roast ducks and clotted
cream, and with the best smuggled brandy
besides, till I cried ' Hold, enough ! ' but they
would rather let me bleed them till they were
faint, than part with a shilling."

" Then why ask them for money ? "

" Because it is my duty. I wish to establish
a subscription-list for the Church Missionary
Society ; and as you intend calling on the
farmers, I would rather wait on them at the
same time."

" Have you got a spare cassock, my dear
father, that I could wear ? " said George,
laughing.

" It is because you are as unlike a priest

as possible," said his father, enjoying his pleasantry, " that I hope my own presence will be
less insufferable."

The old gentleman was proud of his son,
and proud of his promotion; and, moreover,
thought it would be good policy to press
the subscription-list when the farmers were
placable—as he believed they would be—at
the sight of Captain Millett, fresh from his
new-made honours.

Mr. Millett did not overrate the pleasure of
the rustics at seeing their old friend, who
had grown up among them from a boy; and
the policy of pressing for subscriptions at the
same time, was, in the general, a successful
move; but at one farmhouse neither the
presence of the sailor nor the eloquence of
the parson could unbutton the breeches-
pocket.

Farmer Gripe had saved up, by industry
and frugality, a comfortable little hoard, which
he intended for his own peculiar benefit. He
paid all legitimate. demands upon him with
unswerving punctuality, but he was never
known to subscribe for any purpose, either
benevolent or religious. Mr. Millett endeavoured to break through this undeviating rule,

and commenced his assault on Mr. Gripe by depicting the miseries and ignorance of the heathen, which discourse was patiently heard to an end; and after the good clergyman had expressed a hope that he should have the assistance of Mr. Gripe, he waited for a reply.

"'Twan't do, Maister Millett, 'twant do."

"I hope you will give me something, Mr. Gripe."

"'Twan't do, Maister Millett, 'twan't do."

"Now, only see what Mr. Snell and Mr. Rowse have given."

"'Twan't do, 'twan't do," said the farmer, shaking his head.

"See what I have given myself," said the parson, showing from the bag a five pound note.

"His, his; but how do I knaw you wan't take un out again? 'Twan't do, 'twan't do."

At this reply, the whole three had a merry laugh together; Mr. Gripe pluming himself that he was up to a little clerical manœuvring, while the Milletts were amused at his crafty but absurd suspicion. For many a year after George would close up his friendly disputes with his father, with, "'Twan't do."

The day after the conversation with George

Millett, Mrs. Kelly went to Penwith, and had a private interview with Lucy.

"George Millett is returned from sea," she said, when they were closeted together; "and I have seen him, and it is at his request that I have called here to-day."

"Is he well?"

"He is very well, and has been promoted to the rank of commander."

"That only gives me pleasure," said Lucy, "because it pleases him. I have often thought if we had both been poor we should have had less trouble; and, with our energies, and the wide world before us, we could not fail to push our way in the world. But it is vain to talk of circumstances we could wish for; we must take our lot as it falls. Did you tell him that I felt he was throwing away his prospects in life by waiting for me?"

"Yes, my dear; but I believe as long as you wait, George will wait."

"Then, Mrs. Kelly, he will wait till I marry him, or wait till I die. I can never marry another. I love him, and more than love him. I honour him, that he has never made an attempt to induce me to swerve from my duty. I feel proud of the affection of a

high-spirited, honourable man, who, for my
sake, can subject himself to the unreasonable
prejudices of my father—who must despise
the peculiarities of my sect — and who yet
neglects the opportunities of a more ambitious
alliance. On the other hand, I have no other
course to pursue. I am bound by nature, duty,
and religion, to submit myself to the kindest
father that treads the surface of this wide
world. He has tempted me, with projects
of affluence, to unite myself to some of his
wealthy connexions, who would hold George
Millett's position, with his father's gentility,
in contempt; but in my education I have
been unrestrained in my tastes and feelings,
and they do not sympathize with the dull and
methodical system that the Friends inculcate.
I hope much from the kindness of my dear
old father; but as long as he forbids our union
he shall be obeyed, if it cost me a broken
heart and an early grave!"

The latter part of this speech was spoken
with emotion, and Lucy could not restrain her
tears. Mrs. Kelly waited a few minutes to
give her time to recover, for she knew, with a
mind so well balanced, whose emotions were
kept in check by well exercised restraint, it

must be deep and strong feeling that disturbed her usual composure.

"I know," said Mrs. Kelly, at length, "how sensible and kind a father you have; and I also know what misgiving he must entertain for your happiness by an alliance with a man whose occupation is war, and what a struggle he must undergo in yielding to a course in opposition to the confirmed principles of a long life. But George begs that you will allow him to see your father, or to write to him. He is impressed with the feeling that a truthful statement will at least mitigate his hostility."

"George has a right to ask it," said Lucy. "The persistent affection of a truthful man for so long a period is a strong argument, but I have not much confidence in its effect. Ask him, instead, to write to me; and I will show the letter to my father, and will add my own entreaties that he will give it an indulgent consideration. Unfortunately, at the present time the Church is in more than usual disfavour."

"What has occurred that could increase his animosity to the Church?"

"In the first place, the attempts of Parson

Wilkins, as he calls him, to lay the spirits that haunt the neighbourhood of Trelaggan Church, have excited his ridicule and contempt. But the most serious cause is that he has lost a large sum of money by the forgeries of that Mr. Blackmore, who lately served the parish of Leyland."

"Forgeries, do you say?"

"Yes; the day after the Visitation Court he packed up all the valuables in his possession and decamped; and, as he is an entire cheat, the bills that he has discounted at my father's bank must be forgeries."

"Then Miss Treloar has lost her lover?"

"Yes; or, rather, she has escaped being married to a wicked man. I am very sorry for poor Mary's disappointment and mortification, but that is much the less of the two evils."

Mrs. Kelly spent the remainder of the day at Mr. Weston's, and having arranged that George should address his application to Lucy, she left in the evening for Tredart.

CHAPTER IV.

THE circumstances related by Lucy had, indeed, caused Jonathan Weston to feel additional animosity against the Prelatical Church.

The parish of Leyland was situated in the midst of the exciting scenes we have undertaken to relate. About half-way up a mountainous ascent, on the borders of the cliff, stood the church, with its ivy-mantled tower, looking over a bay that terminated in a beach surrounded by lofty hills.

The interior of the ancient fabric was ornamented with carved work of the most fanciful devices, and, except here and there the head of a cherub had been struck off, was in a wonderful state of preservation. The massive granite pillars, each hewn out of a solid block, were marvels of labour and cost; for the church was very distant from those granite hills that produced them, and the contrivances that could bring them up over those high steeps, and down the deep valleys, again to re-ascend, baffle conjecture.

The screen separating the chancel from the nave was perfect, and the panels of the open pews were adorned with the armorial bearings of many a Cornish family that had ceased to exist.

The tower was not a part of the church and constructed at the western end, as is usual, but was detached, and situated on the south. The lower part of it was hewn out of the rock, and the upper part was built of solid masonry. It was connected with the church by a covered way, the entrance to which was through a Gothic arch on either side. The tower could not be ascended from the basement, but there was an entrance from the churchyard above to the first floor. Altogether, the church and tower were peculiar in their situation, and equally singular in their construction.

It is not wonderful that in a superstitious age such a fabric, situated in a wild and lonely place, should have the reputation of a haunted church. From the churchyard also many strange sights had been seen, and sounds heard, and few ventured alone in that neighbourhood in the darkness of night.

At some distance from the church was a decayed old-fashioned mansion, only partially occupied, whose spacious hall, grand staircase, wide passages, and large and almost empty rooms, were suitable places of resort for restless spirits; while its secluded situation, surrounded by old moss-grown trees, moaning and whistling with every blast, in the dead of night afforded an appropriate accompaniment to their dismal visitations.

Sometimes, when the hour of midnight had passed, a coach-and-four were heard to drive up to the front entrance, and when the servants hastened from their beds to admit the visitors, there was nothing to be seen. At other times, the former proprietors were supposed to revisit the scenes of their mirth, and the clashing of glasses and the tramp of feet were heard in the banqueting-hall; and they have been known to enter with a gust of wind, scamper with rapidity through the passages of the house, and be heard of no more.

This was supposed to be the occupation of departed spirits, who, disturbed on account of their own crimes, or desirous to punish by their nocturnal visits the crimes of persons still lingering in the flesh, revisit, in their spiritual form, the scenes of their former existence.

The Reverend Ralph Wilkins, who served the church of a neighbouring parish, with the aid of another learned clerk, undertook to exorcise these troubled and troublesome spirits, and to confine them for ever to the regions below. But it appeared that they were only pretenders to the occult science, for although they used their incantations at midnight, and spoke loud enough for any listening spirits to hear, they failed to make their appearance.

"*Glen.* I can call spirits from the vasty deep.
    Hot. But will they come when you do call
            for them?"

It was asserted that ghosts still made their appearance at the mansion, and strange sights were seen in the churchyard, and that the well-meant efforts of Mr. Wilkins had been without effect.

Persons passing near the church had seen, in gloomy nights, figures moving among the tombs. Others had seen a pallid light suddenly appear, and again vanish, and then again start up from another part of the burial-ground, as if from the grave.

Well-credited persons had witnessed sights of an unearthly character, and after night-fall the highway by the church was universally avoided.

There were some few, who kept their own council, that were acquainted with the cause of these nocturnal appearances. The first floor of the tower, by the collusion of the sexton, was not unfrequently filled with kegs of brandy, and their stowage and removal required dark nights. The doorway being hidden from almost every side, as we have already shown, offered a communication both secret and safe; and the loopholes of the tower were concealed from the view of travellers by the intervention of the church. Therefore no glare was ever seen from the tower; but the lurid reflection of the light from the tomb-stones and the grassy hillocks around, and the dark figures of the smugglers, stalking like spectres among the graves, scared the emissaries of the Government from a neighbourhood of such frightful visitations.

There was no one who held the pretensions of "Parson Wilkins" in greater contempt than Mr. Weston, who ridiculed, as preposterous, the virtues that a regular priesthood was said to possess.

But if the ghost-laying added bitterness to an animosity that was before sufficiently strong, it was surpassed by the escapade of Mr. Blackmore.

This was the gentleman that Lucy described, in her early acquaintance with Mrs. Kelly, as paying his addresses to Miss Treloar.

The incumbent, living far away in the West, had engaged Mr. Blackmore as the curate of Leyland church.

This divine seemed to have taken upon himself the duties of his profession, more for the sake of occupation than for the purpose of emolument. His means appeared to be ample, his manners agreeable, his information extensive, and his varied talents of a high order.

He resided at the vicarage-house in a style far beyond the expenditure his stipend would permit; but that rather added to his respectability and credit, because it favoured the supposition that his inheritance was large.

The notoriety of his remarkable eloquence drew crowds to the church; and although novelty often draws a congregation that familiarity will disperse, its usual effect in this case was not apparent, for the pressure in the aisles was never so great as when his last sermon was preached.

His personal appearance corresponded with his mental attainments. He was intellectually handsome, and he dressed with exquisite taste.

He was *fêted* by the neighbouring gentry, and his acquaintance was sought by every one who could aspire to the dignity. As might have been expected, the provident mothers of marriageable daughters made him welcome; nor did they conceal the happiness that might be in store for any one that might be blest with the delight to be derived from the accomplishments of their Julianas or Arabellas.

The fillies were trotted out, but, sooth to say, their allurements were not fascinating. He at length set all machinations at rest, by showing a decided preference for one that had shown no anxiety for his favour.

This was Miss Treloar, the friend of Miss Weston; and, if personal appearance and keen and lively wit were objects of value, she merited the choice.

It cannot be denied that, before any lengthened wooing had taken place, the fascinations of this young curate had affected the heart of Mary Treloar. It may have been that she was proud of a preference to which all the other young ladies were aspiring; it is certain she was charmed, as well as others, with his agreeable society. He danced and sang in a style that surpassed the *élite* of the country town, and his reading, especially of Shakespeare, was unsurpassed.

The upshot of all this singing and dancing and reading was, that Miss Treloar and Mr. Blackmore were engaged to be married; and the happy event was to take place in the course of the ensuing spring.

But in this changeable world many things unexpectedly happen, and many events, anticipated with certainty, never occur.

The popularity of the Reverend Reginald Blackmore, the officiating minister of Leyland, was unabated.

A charity sermon was to be preached, and a special charity sermon by so gifted a minister was not to be disregarded.

On the appointed Sunday the parish church was full, and fortunate were the persons who arrived early enough to obtain standing-room in the aisles. The text selected for the occasion was most appropriate: "Whoso hath this world's good, and seeth his brother have need, and shutteth up his bowels of compassion from him, how dwelleth the love of God in him?"

A most powerful discourse followed. The whole congregation was affected—many persons were in tears.

The usual result of a good sermon for a charitable object was obtained; and the wealthy, whose consciences had been awakened, evinced their sincerity by handsome donations. So far all went well.

But the Archdeacon's Court was held in an inland town in the course of the following week, when, as usual, the names of the clergy were called over. Among others the name of Reginald Blackmore was called, and his licence to serve Leyland Church demanded. He had left it at home, but would produce it on the following day.

No suspicion was aroused among the bystanders in consequence of so natural an accident, and the archdeacon made no comment on the irregularity.

But the day following was otherwise employed. On that day the Reverend Reginald

Blackmore packed almost everything that was valuable at the parsonage and deserted his home, taking with him all that was portable, even the proceeds of the collection that was intended for the benefit of the poor.

When the sudden and suspicious departure of the clergyman became known, a large number of persons he had patronized by his preference were in a state of dismay. Bills of exchange were floating in great numbers that had no other security than the name of Reginald Blackmore. Large amounts were due to the draper, the grocer, and the butcher; and a legion of other creditors, from the wine-merchant to the stationer, learnt, with bitter disappointment, the loss of their customer and their goods.

When the consternation of the first surprise had subsided, and the deluded tradesmen began to consider what means could be adopted to mitigate their loss, they found that by the disappearance of the defaulter, they had no legal means of seizing his person or goods. It occurred to them that what the law did not provide for, they might decree for themselves, and proceeding to the vicarage, at which there was free entrance, began to take possession, each on his own account, of everything they could carry off. They sacked the house from the garret to the cellar.

A very valuable horse was ridden off from the stable, and the smallest utensil from the scullery was carried away. There was a general scramble, and a perfect clearance.

The noble matrons of Penwith, who had angled, in behalf of their daughters, to catch the spruce clergyman, now gossipped together, and—wise after the event—said they always suspected that there was something amiss; while the young ladies themselves—piqued, at the time, that their own charms were neglected and the preference given to another—now pitied poor Mary Treloar, although they felt obliged to confess she had been a *little* too forward.

Thus, as it often happens in this disappointing and deceitful world, the winner of the prize was the most unfortunate, and the spleen of the conquered was gratified by an ample revenge.

The fugitive parson could not be found. No one had been seen resembling his person, and he had left no trace of his footsteps behind. The nine days' wonder died away, and the late curate of Leyland was spoken of historically. Years passed by, and the angry feelings of injured creditors had waxed cold.

At length a letter arrived to the chief constable of the hundred, directing him to send some one to the governor of Bristol gaol to identify the person of the Reverend Reginald Blackmore, formerly of the parish of Leyland, in the county of Cornwall.

The mandate was complied with, and a tradesman, holding his dishonoured acceptance, to whom that gentleman was personally known, proceeded to Bristol.

A number of prisoners were led out before him, but he had no difficulty in pointing out the man.

There stood Mr. Blackmore, charged, in the name of James Wilkinson, *alias* Samuel White, with sundry forgeries to a large amount. The fox was hunted down at last. He had begun a business from which there is no retirement, and a few months after he hung from the gallows outside the walls of Bristol gaol.

The person from Cornwall was not summoned for the purpose of conviction, but of tracing the history of that remarkable man. He began life as a stage-player. He had never been bred to the Church, or been ordained. He lived, by personating many characters, on the hard-won gains of other people.

When Mrs. Kelly supplicated, on behalf of Captain Millett, that another application should be made to Mr. Weston, the disappearance of the counterfeit curate had just occurred, and Lucy regretted the circumstance, because it was a scandal against the Church, and might also irritate her father on account of his pecuniary loss. But Jonathan Weston, faithful to his principles, took no part in the pursuit of the fugitive priest, because a successful prosecution must end with the gallows.

"If," said he to a fellow-sufferer, "I have been the dupe of my credulity, my property must suffer, and I have no desire to add to the penalty, or to gratify my revenge by the commission of sin. There is a higher law than that framed by Act of Parliament, that teaches thee to do good to them that despitefully use thee; and my opinion is that the gallows is not the good that was intended. He deserves it, thou wilt say; but thou wilt hardly find executioners enough for all that deserve it."

"I agree with the law," said Mr. Rawlings.

"A man that cheats the public, like this Black-more, ought to be hanged."

"I should like," said the Quaker, "to hear thee talk less about *that* cheat, and more about *others* that the law does *not* hang. A messenger from thy priest hath been at my house this morning demanding tithes, which I refused to pay him, and he hath taken. away sundry articles to be sold. It was quite right for thee to pay him, because thou hast doubtless digested the many silly things he hath told thee; but I have neither employed him, nor had the value of his discourse, and I am sorry to see that thou art ready to hang Reginald Blackmore, and willing to give the other miscreants licence to rob me."

"It is the law," replied Mr. Rawlings, "and we must obey the law."

"If thy law is opposed to the law of the Bible, James Rawlings, I think I would *rather* obey the Bible. Dost not thou believe that thy priests might be better employed than in riding about the country in dark nights laying ghosts?"

"No; I don't think they could. The coach-and-four that used to drive up to Kilmarth has never been there since Parson Wilkins laid it."

"Then Parson Wilkins can lay a ghost of any size?" said the Quaker, smiling. "I should have thought the four prancing horses rather too much for him. Didn't I hear that the carrier and his wife were frightened by a ghost?"

"Yes, at the foot of Deer-park hill; and they have not been well since."

"Canst thou tell me when the ghost appeared?"

"On Thursday night, about ten o'clock. Many persons are afraid to go by that road, and Mr. Wilkins is going to lay the troubled spirit. It was like a man looking over a gate. It neither moved nor spoke."

"In returning that night from Tregarth," said Mr. Weston, "where I had been transacting some business with my friend Zechariah Drew, that kept me later than usual, I saw at that place what appeared to be a man looking over the gate, and I discovered that it was the shadow of a pollard tree, caused by the moonlight. If thou wilt ask Farmer Honey to fell that tree, he will effectually lay the ghost, and save Parson Wilkins the trouble."

CHAPTER V.

WHEN Lascare wrote the letter to his wife, which was read to Miss Weston, his vessel was at Crosaix, lying beside the quay. The man referred to in that letter, who was seen daily prowling about the neighbourhood, and taking particular notice of the Swift, was a source of anxiety to the crew. They conceived that he was a spy of the English Government; and that when the departure of their vessel took place, information of that circumstance would be forwarded to his employers.

They rightly conjectured that the preparations made to receive them on their last voyage had been the result of this person's report. From information conveyed to them by letter, they learned the sad consequences that had attended the signal which saved them from a dangerous encounter; and although they had adopted a system for signals—which had been arranged in England, and of which they were advised by post—that would be free from danger, and equally sure, they took precautions by which they would be enabled to resist a hostile attack, if any should be made.

It was no part of their policy to proceed *vi et armis*, but to elude their pursuers, unless they were brought into contact with an insignificant foe. Although Lascare had furnished the Swift from the armoury of the privateer, being apprehensive that danger might occur, he also provided himself at Crosaix with other materials of war.

Whether phrenologists have discovered or not to what peculiar passions the individuals of the human race are addicted, it is certain that each is carried forward by the current of his desires.

" For I had heard of battles, and I longed
To follow to the field some warlike lord."

The Peace Society would have bound the aspiring hero hand and foot, and cast him into prison; and yet young Norval was gentle, generous, and kind.

The captain of the Swift was not a man to be daunted by a slight obstruction, for he was as resolute in danger as he was mild and benevolent on other occasions. Taking advantage of settled weather, and a favourable wind, he set sail, and in a few days came in sight of the Cornish coast.

Again the Swift stood " off and on " in the distance, and again the smugglers on the lookout became aware of her arrival. It was an anxious time. Although the coastguard had, as yet, no positive information that the Swift had sailed, the Government had apprised them that she was ready for sea, and might be daily expected. They therefore again made every preparation for a seizure.

The men were required to do double duty —the distances from each other were duly arranged — and every hour information was passed from man to man, relating to the occurrences of the night. The island was closely watched ; and that—formerly the safest of places — was become the most dangerous. Every man was equipped with loaded carbine and pistols, and the short naval sword hung by his side.

All these menacing preparations were noticed by the smugglers ; and having taken council together, they determined that the signal " to keep off" should again be made. There was, at this time, no danger in making the signal; because, while it would be equally effectual, it was some distance from the sea.

Again, in the darkness of the night, a blazing fire was kindled, which could be distinctly seen by several men stationed on eminences near the coast, without having the power to suppress it. This, however, informed them that the cruiser was off the coast.

The night passed without any other event, and the following day was spent by both parties as if nothing had occurred. The signal was of ambiguous import to the coast-guard, for they were unable to discover whether it boded a landing or a postponement; whether the Swift was intended to take another destination, or to wait for a more favourable opportunity. It therefore became necessary that night after night they should be prepared for any emergency, and a very harassing duty succeeded.

But the captain of the smuggler understood that there was danger to be apprehended by approaching the shore; and consequently he sailed at a distance during the day, and approached the land in the darkness of the night.

For more than a week Lascare endured this state of perplexity, waiting in vain for the expected signal; while his associates on the shore deemed that any attempt to land would be attended with the greatest calamity.

One dark night—anxious for the desired signal—he approached the coast; and cruising before the small towns that dotted the sea-board, he saw the lights glimmering from the houses that were nearest the coast. He sailed close to the mouth of Tregarth, and fancied he could see the light from the little casement of Edith's cottage, which stood high above the town; but the vessel glided by, and he lost sight of the home he dared not enter.

He watched the different promontories of the coast, the fresh breeze from the north filling the sails, and carrying the fleet sloop along at a rapid pace, but there was no signal, and the night was wearing away.

Soon the hours of the morning were coming in. The hope of the night was giving place to weariness and disappointment. The wind now scarcely filled the sails, but the little vessel moved steadily on.

"The wind's dying away," said Ned Allen, the mate.

"Then," said the captain, "keep her head to sea."

She veered around, but the change of her course diminished her speed, and the sailors asked each other if she moved. Soon there was no doubt. A dead calm had set in. The loose sails hung down in folds, and the vessel sat motionless on the water.

In this precarious situation, the crew were filled with alarm. Hour after hour wore away, and the longed-for breeze delayed its coming. The dawn of morning came on, and found them embayed within a headland that stretched far to the south.

Within one mile of the shore, within view from many a port, was the cruiser, the hoped-for prize of every station, as motionless on the water as when she lay on the stocks before she glided to the unknown destinies of the greedy sea.

Until daylight came, Lascare kept his own counsel. When all hope of a light wind that might come in with the morning was gone, he called his men together, and made them fully acquainted with the danger he apprehended.

"Now," said he, "the time is come that will

show what stuff we are made of. Nothing can save us if we haven't the spirit of men. There's no cutter near, but the Preventive boats will put off as soon as they see us from the shore. I've made up my mind. Before they take the Swift, they shall take my life. They can show no force that can conquer us, but if there's any that would rather go to prison than fight, if there's a coward in the crew, let him go below. No man shall fight against his will. We have to choose whether we shall have our freedom, or whether the land-sharks that have been waiting for us so long shall find a prize in the Swift, and a prison for the crew."

The men, four in number, looked to the mate for a reply. They had talked together on their situation, and had resolved that if the captain determined on defending the vessel, he should be supported with all the energy that four resolute men could give.

Bold, brave men were the men of Tregarth. They were the sons of Nature's aristocracy, and the fathers of noble men, for to this day they are as dauntless as the generations that preceded them.

Accustomed to the exercise of their courage and skill, peril was their pastime, and

"When the tempest scowl'd, they scowl'd the tempest."

Edward Allen was about the same age as Lascare.

They had fished together, and sailed together, and were messmates in the privateer. Lascare had a strong regard for him, and valued him highly, both for his courage and skill.

The mate stood forward as the spokesman for the crew.

"We've made up our minds, cap'n, to stan' by you. We didn't think that you wus goin' to give in; and before theise lazy, lubberly devils shall put a second hand upon the bulwarks of the Swift, they'll drop into the sey. We'll give 'em the chance to try swimmin' with won paw."

The others declared that they would rather fight than go to prison.

"Shell I git up the arms?" said Allen.

"No, not yet," replied Lascare. "I've known the day, Ned, when I was more ready for fighting. When we took the brig, off

Alderney, I was longing for the fray, and we buckled on our cutlasses an hour before they were wanted. But 'tisn't against the enemies of our country that we shall do battle to-day. I shan't fight with less determination, but I shall begin with more reluctance. Till the fellows show themselves, let the arms alone. A breeze may start up at any time. For once I wish the Swift was like a soap-chest, for then they might take her for a coaster. But I may soon be glad that she is less like a chest, and more like herself. Let a light breeze spring up, we'll steal away from them like a witch."

The sun rose gently, with a fiery redness, over the headland, and illumined one vast canopy of the clearest blue.

The sea, reflecting the brightness of the sky from its glassy surface, was without motion or sound, not even the ripple that sometimes fringes the shore on a peaceful day seemed to disturb the universal repose.

The island, crowned with the hoary ruins of the ancient church, lay floating in the watery mirror, and casting a lengthened shadow to the west. The brown and rugged rocks were stripped of their splashing foam, and the hol-

lows and caverns had lost the gurgling sound
of the rushing wave.

On the higher rocks, that jutted furthest
towards the sea, stood the sea-gulls, the divers,
and the cormorants, mingled peacefully together, with their heads turned towards the
south, as if viewing the motionless vessels that
floated in the distance. All nature was in the
enjoyment of tranquillity and peace.

Lascare stood on the deck of his vessel,
anxiously watching the shore. At one time a
mist floated from the eastward, and promised
a friendly concealment; but as the sun rose
higher the air again became clear, and again
he watched the harbour of Penwith.

Although they were within one mile of
the shore, they were seven miles from the
nearest port. Three miles further west was
the harbour of Tregarth, and further to the
west the coast-guard were watching at every
creek.

At times, as a boat jutted out from the
harbour, the crew imagined that they were
descried; but again they felt relief as it moved
in the direction of the fishing-ground, or
stretched away towards the west.

As the morning wore on, they thought the

vessel had been taken for a trading-smack, which was a class common on the coast, and they breathed more freely. Good fortune might send them a breeze; or, if they remained unperceived till nightfall, an off-land current might waft them from the shore.

The smugglers of Tregarth, watching from the hills, knew the tackle of their own craft before the sun glistened on her sails, and there was scarcely less anxiety on the shore than agitated the minds of the crew. With the greatest circumspection they lingered at their different posts, and neither by gesture, nor for the purpose of informing their colleagues of the danger that threatened, was there any indication of alarm.

Amidst all this uncertainty, Lascare remained on the watch with undeviating resolution, hoping for a release; but determined, if necessary, to defend the vessel and cargo to the last extremity, whatever might be the result.

He watched the harbour of Penwith—the nearest port; and if, from weariness, his eyes turned on any other object, they found their way back again in the direction of the expected foe.

He took out his watch—it was ten o'clock. How long the minutes were! At this time one of the younger men called attention to an object moving beyond the Mewstone. Lascare looked through the glass.

"That," said he, coolly, as if the pain of uncertainty was dispelled, "is the Preventive boat of Tregarth, with the jack flying at her stern. I should be sorry to injure you, Mr. Collins" (still keeping his eye fixed to the glass), "but you can't have the Swift. The Tregarth officer is wider awake than the man at Penwith. If you pull like that, my men, you will come breathless on a bootless errand."

He said this aloud to himself, and for the benefit of the crew; and there being now no uncertainty about the matter, he went aft, and sat composedly at the stern.

Scarcely ten minutes had elapsed before the boat from Penwith also made her appearance, carrying the union jack, and making straight for the Swift.

When she had come more into the open, the crews of the two boats saw each other, and simultaneously stripped; but the Penwith boat, though last at sea, was a mile in advance of her competitor, and was stretching her way with full swing towards the bay.

"Now, my men, said Lascare, "let them see what stuff we are made of. There need be no hurry. Keep the sails set, and let every man do his work quietly. There they come on. They see each other now, and are disappointed that the prize must be shared, unless one boat can arrive soon enough to cheat the other of his half. Now they strip, and pull like men greedy for plunder."

"There's another boat out," cried Ned Allen. "The Kenmouth boat. We'm enough for 'em all. Let 'em come on. They won't go back so jolly. Now, cap'n, we see the wust, let's knaw what to do, and we'll make ready."

"This last boat makes matters more even," said Lascare. "The odds were too much in our favour before. In the first place, hoist the black flag; they will then see that we shall not be the sugar-plum they expected. Not this time shall the prize satisfy the hungry craving of these greedy sharks. Now bring up the arms."

While the sailors were below, preparing the arms, the man who defied the Government,

and whose skill and daring had as yet been
unmatched, paced the deck, keeping his eye
on the boats that were approaching, with the
design of making a formidable prize.

He was a man of ordinary size, but of sym-
metrical proportions; of great physical power,
but it was derived more from muscular develop-
ment and energy of character, than from weight.
His complexion was swarthy; his curling hair
and piercing eyes were black; and the whole
facial appearance denoted an extraction that
had neither a Celtic nor a Saxon root.

Tradition had connected him with a family
that, centuries before, had emigrated from
Spain, relying on the protection of a noble
soldier, who had won his laurels under the
auspices of

" Old John of Gaunt
  Time-honoured Lancaster."

But there was nothing authentic on record
of this gossiping report; and the descendant of
the hero of the Spanish wars, though believing
the tale, could find no documentary evidence
in the archives of his house to prove the descent of Lascare.

Whatever clime was the home of his ancestors, it was certain that he was an exotic in this; and neither time nor intermarriage had defaced the distinctive marks of foreign extraction.

As he paced the deck, watching his approaching foes, he formed plans of resistance suitable to any form of attack that might be adopted; and when the sailors returned to the deck, bearing the weapons they were ordered to use, they perceived a change in the demeanour of their captain. They had seen the same aspect before in trying emergencies, and it betokened confidence, resolution, and command.

The eyes were sunk deeper under the brow; the lips were compressed; the foot was planted with firmness; and the orders were given in a tone of authority that compelled instant obedience.

When this mood was on the commander, an Eastern despot would envy the servility that waited on Lascare.

The arms were placed on the deck in the number and order that had been directed, and the crew looked, rather than asked, for further commands.

"In the first place," said the captain, "let

every man load for himself four carbines, and see that his flints are in good order. There must be nothing left to chance. Every shot must tell. Take a reserve of cartridges in case of need. Above all, keep yourselves cool and steady."

Each man loaded his carbines, buckled his cutlass to his side, and placed a brace of loaded pistols in his belt.

CHAPTER VI.

WHILE the arms were being prepared on board the vessel, the three boats were dashing over the tranquil sea, and, inspired by the example of each other, were straining to get as early as possible to their destination.

The officers observed the black flag hanging from the mast-head of the Swift with some surprise, and the wind failing to float it, Lascare had sent a sailor to extend its folds to their full length, that they might be fully warned of the danger awaiting them.

Lieutenant Yarnall, who commanded the foremost boat, regarded this as the bravado of a buccaneer; but the officer from Tregarth, with a more intimate knowledge of the character of Lascare, viewed the defiance with apprehension.

Early in the morning, his men had descried a suspicious-looking craft becalmed within the head, and they called his attention to the peculiarity of her hull.

The long clipper-like shape—the length of mast, and clean equipment—corresponded with the information the Government had forwarded as the characteristics of the Swift; and these indications, combined with the notice given, that she had sailed, and the signal the smugglers had made, convinced the lieutenant that the long-hoped-for prize was at hand.

He hastily manned the boat, taking care that the crew should be armed with cutlasses and pistols, and proceeded to sea with the exultation of a huntsman having his game in view.

When the boat had passed a tongue of land that had for some time concealed her, she came in sight of the crew from Penwith, and their recognition was a mutual disappointment.

The Penwith boat was at least a mile ahead, and, although the last to take the sea, would be the first to arrive. To add to the mortification of both, the Kenmouth boat hove in sight, and, although the latter had less chance, an accident might make her also a sharer in the prize.

The three boats were in full speed, excited by all the eagerness of a race.

Nothing daunted by the black flag, Yarnall made straight for the sloop, and the crisis was imminent. His crew had the usual arms, but he conceived that the show of his authority, backed by the force of the coming boats, was sufficient.

Lascare stood at the stern, watching his approaching foes. Finding that the exhibition of the black flag had no effect, he ordered his men to stand on the western side, with their carbines resting on the bulwarks, in the hope that a further show of hostility would prevent an engagement; but the rash Lieutenant, greedy for his prey, and fearing that postponement, by giving the others time to come up, would lessen the value of his share of the prize, urged on his men.

A shot was fired from the Swift, passing near Yarnall's head, but designedly aimed to miss him. It had no effect; the Lieutenant shouted, "On, boys, on!" Another shot; the bow oar dropped from the man's hand, and the man himself fell forward from his seat.

Yarnall now ordered the starboard men to hold hard, that he might turn the boat out of danger. This was allowed. The whole crew might have been dead men in less time than it has taken to tell it, but no order had been given. No more shots were fired, and the boat was placed beyond range. It was a timely movement, or the Lieutenant himself would have paid the penalty of his contempt for the smuggler.

The crew of the sloop still remained standing with their pointed carbines, while Lascare coolly reloaded those discharged.

Yarnall now went forward to the bow to see what had been the effect of the shot. The man was dead. The ball, piercing his back, had entered his lungs, and he died instantly.

They now rowed gently back to meet the coming boats. The Tregarth men were the first to arrive. Lieutenant Collins's usually good-humoured countenance had a serious aspect.

"Look," said Yarnall, "at what that blood-thirsty villain has done! We must pay him off when the Kenmouth boat comes up."

"As to paying off," said Collins, "we will consult about that when Newman arrives; but if the smuggler had been a bloodthirsty man, you would not have been alive to tell it. It may be that being nearer, and eager to board, you did not observe all that I saw; but I must do the fellow the justice to say that he did everything he could to prevent a collision. He hoisted that black flag, and, fearing it might escape our notice, he sent a man to unfold it. He placed his men in line, and showed their carbines on the bulwarks. I saw through the glass that every man had his cutlass buckled on, with a brace of pistols in his belt. One man fired his piece that the ball might whistle in your ear and be harmless. I saw the shot fall into the water, and it showed that you were within reach. You went on. He next fired at your bow man, whose misfortune shows that his aim is sure. You turned your boat, and the piece that was raised to his shoulder was instantly lowered. If he had directed his crew to fire, not a man of you would be left alive. If he feared us all united, he would, in the first place, have demolished your crew. No; he is a lawless and reckless, but, I must do him the justice to say, not a bloodthirsty man."

By this time the Kenmouth boat arrived, and an earnest consultation ensued. Yarnall, whose cupidity led him to attack the cruiser alone, and whose impetuosity had brought misfortune to his crew, seemed the only one unconscious that he owed his life to the forbearance of his foe. He urged a joint attack, and a sudden boarding by the three crews at once.

"A spirited onslaught," he said, "will strike them with terror. We are now twenty-one well-armed men against five."

"As to striking them with terror," said Newman, "it will take more than human power to strike with terror the man that opened upon you. I watched all the proceedings with my glass. He took up the carbines, one after the other, with as much coolness and deliberation as if he was engaged in an ordinary shooting match. When he had knocked over your man, he proceeded to take another piece; and I believe that he alone, in the position he occupied, was more than a match for you all. Why the others didn't fire I don't know, seeing we are three of us, but the lives of your crew were at the mercy of the smugglers."

"Yarnall," said Collins, emboldened by the support he had received from Newman, "you are the senior officer, and I place myself under your command. If your orders are to attack the vessel, I will obey, but you will not live to bear the responsibility of your act. Before we reach the sloop, one half of us will be dead, and the other half will attempt to board with the cutlass and pistol at their heads. Even if we had suitable weapons, men cannot pull and fight at the same time, but they will offer their broad backs a point blank shot to the enemy. I am bound to obey you, and, except for my little ones, my life is of small value; but it is my duty to tell you that the course you recommend is not fighting, but murder."

"I also," said Newman, "protest against any further attempt. I am under your orders, Yarnall, but, if you should survive the fray, I hold you responsible for all the consequences that may result."

The conference ended in a determination to abandon the prize, and each took his course to his own port.

The smugglers retired from their menacing attitude, and replaced their weapons, and sat longing for a propitious breeze before any more formidable foe might appear.

While these movements were taking place in the bay, the people of Tregarth became acquainted with the perilous position of the Swift. The hills were crowded with spectators, and at the appearance of fire-arms they became greatly excited.

Edith had been apprised early in the day of the critical position of her husband, and the wonted spirit of former years returned. She climbed the hill with one of Lascare's trusted associates, and, reaching the top, stood at the elbow of her friend to learn the changes that every minute produced. The practised eye of the veteran detected every movement, and he related all the occurrences with the glass constantly fixed to his sight.

Now Edith wished Heaven had made her a man, to stand by Richard. She thought nothing of danger, and loved the daring intrepidity of Lascare. Woman as she was, she longed to be there. She could load, she could supply arms, and tell the noble hero how she loved his daring spirit; she could bid defiance to the wretched robbers; she could stand before him, and ward off the blow. Why was she not there?

While these things were passing through her mind, the boats were stealing nearer to the sloop; and now the men of Penwith appeared close to the hull. The smoke of fire-arms appeared.

" The fight's begun," said the old sailor;
" they'm firing from the Swift."

Edith stood breathless to hear more.

" There's only five oars pullin'. One man's
shot. They'm backing astern. No more firin'.
Oh, Dick! There you're wrong, my boy.
You should knock 'em down when you got
'em."

" No, James, Richard isn't wrong," exclaimed Edith, in a complaining tone, now
considerably subdued on hearing that the
boat was retreating. " Richard doesn't want
to kill the men, but only to keep his own
property."

" But he should finish off this boat fust,"
said the old man. " There's two more to come
up, and 'tis easier work to take won at a
time."

" What are they doing now, James ?"

" Why, they'm got out of fire, and they'm
waitin' for the other boats to come op."

" And will they all three attack Richard ?"

" I don't know what they'll do; but if they
try that they'll have a hard fight. Now they'm
all together, the three starns be touchin', the
officers be havin' a talk."

Edith waited a few minutes, and then

exclaimed, — " How long they are talking !"

Every minute, to Edith, seemed ten, as
she restlessly moved from one side of the
old man to the other, looking into his
face, to see from the expression of his
countenance whether any movement had
taken place, — language was too slow for
her.

Still she waited on, now looking in the
direction of the boats, now into the countenance of the old sailor, and now again asking,
" if anything was doing ?"

" They 'm having a long yarn," said
the old man, "and the more they talk the
less they 'll like fightin'. Now they 'm
movin'."

" Are they going towards the Swift ?"

" Wait—no—every boat is gain' to his own
port. They given ut op. 'Tis all over now,
and I'm glad of ut !"

" And so am I—very glad !" said Edith.

" Now then I think we may go home to
have somethin' to eat."

" Do you go home, James; but I will stay
here. The boats may return, or a breeze may
spring up. If the calm continues, I will watch

till night; and when you come again, bring me a crust of bread."

The old sailor went home for refreshments, and when he returned a light wind from the shore had carried the Swift from the bay, and Edith was watching the canvas when the hull had ceased to appear.

CHAPTER VII.

While the events related in the last chapter were agitating the mind of Edith, other occurrences affecting the future of her friend were taking place at Penwith.

When Mrs. Kelly informed George Millett that Lucy gave her permission that he should address his letter to her, and that she would further it with her own entreaties, a thrill of delight pervaded the young man. To prevent any extravagant hopes, she reminded him of the prejudices of the old Quaker, and expressed a wish that it might not end in disappointment.

"But," said George, full of the hope and enthusiasm of his age, "she must be mine. For three tedious years I have neither seen nor written to her, and she regards me still. It is a great honour, Mrs. Kelly, to be thought worthy of her; and that she will request her father to permit our union, is itself a prize. The steady, warm, and constant affection of such a girl is worth a universe, and I will strive to be worthy of it. If her father again refuse, I will love and wait—I will wait and hope. Even if the grave close over me, having waited in vain, it shall cover a breast whose happiness it has been to be animated with her love, and to have lived in the prospect of a blessing that happens to few."

There were times when Mrs. Kelly had misgivings as to the part she had played between the two lovers, but they were dissipated now. The strong affection, guided by the excellent judgment and filial piety of Lucy, and the continued warm admiration of the noble sailor, convinced her that neither wealth nor honour, nor the fleeting grandeur of the world, could confer the happiness that she hoped would at last reward the constancy of her friends.

After the departure of George Millett for a term of three years' service, and receiving news of him, through Mrs. Kelly, at the arrival of every mail, Lucy gradually recovered her wonted appearance. Her lips regained their freshness, and the pale pink again adorned her beautiful face. The sunny cheerfulness returned, and the whole was blended with that indefinite expression which a cultivated intellect imparts to the delicately-formed features of a lady.

She felt confidence in the impetuous but generous sailor, and felt worthy of his affection, and rested in the hope that revolving time would ultimately reward their constancy. But how many a prize looks certain in the distance that a nearer approach makes it difficult to clutch! At the expiration of the period of his service, anxiety again disturbed her repose, and the conversation she had with Mrs. Kelly added to the perplexity of her position. Doubt and uncertainty produced anxious days and restless nights, and these again afflicted a frame too susceptible of the anguish of the mind.

The watchful eyes of old Rachel soon detected that something was amiss, and without disturbing Lucy by prying into the cause, she ascertained that the naval officer had returned, and concluded that further complications were affecting her young mistress, and undermining the health of a frame that was far from robust.

She resolved to make her discovery known to her master, to give him some advice, and to relieve her own mind from any complicity in a course that might lead to a sorrowful event.

"Master," said she, one day, when he

seemed at leisure to listen to her, "hast thee observed Lucy lately?"

"No; I have observed nothing particular, except that she is not so sprightly as formerly. But she is getting older thou know'st."

"Iīs, she's getting older; but I don't think her years be telling upon her so much as her mind."

"I hope Lucy has no trouble on her mind, Rachel?"

"I'm afraid she hath. Thee didn'st tell me anything about it, and it wasn't my business to inquire, but Lucy told me that thee refused thy consent to her marriage with Paason Millett's son some time ago."

"I did so, but what of that?"

"The young man's come back again from sea; and I'm told that a girl that's once liked un, won't forget un very quickly."

"I have that confidence in my daughter, Rachel," said Mr. Weston, assuming an indignant tone, "that I believe she will not disobey her father, and will do nothing to grieve him."

"And so I believe; but 'tis my duty to tell thee that in obeying her father, she may bring herself to the grave."

"Rachel, I have so bred my daughter that she will make everything succumb to reason; and I have explained to her how incompatible such a union would be, and, although it may have produced disappointment, it is one of the lessons we must all learn."

"'Tis all very true, what thee sayst; but we baant all alike, and there be disappointments that some people can't bear. I wish Lucy would forget the young man, but she doesn't; and I believe that this trouble will bring her to the grave."

"I don't see any reason to change my opinion of the incompatibility, if not wickedness, in consenting to such a union."

"I doant knaw, master, if I'm right or no, but, to my mind, it may be a great sin to kill a person; and if thee goest on in this way, thee'll kill thy daughter."

"Woman," said the old man, in great anger, "to what dost thou tempt me?"

The banker immediately left the room, and Rachel busied herself with redoubled vigour in household affairs, gratified in having "told Jonathan Weston a piece of her mind."

Although the Quaker had abruptly terminated the conversation with Rachel, and resented her interference in his affairs, as beyond her province, her communication made him an unhappy man.

He loved his daughter for herself. He was proud of the beauty of her person, and the cultivation of her mind; and, in addition, he loved her as the relic of an angel in heaven. *He* was going down life's hill, and all his plans for aggrandizement — for, call it what he might, that is what it was—were for her. And now this tender flower, that was the express image of her mother, was fading—was pining in secret melancholy—because he could not ally her to one who, in his opinion, was a man of a false creed, and of a murderous occupation.

Jonathan Weston, steadfastly adhering to the principles in which he had been bred, was in a very painful position.

The day following the conversation with Rachel, a batch of letters was laid on the banker's desk, as was usual after the postal delivery. Among them was one for his daughter. It was short and compact, and was of the thick, smooth, gilt-edged, Bath paper.

There was a fashion, even then, that was

adopted by persons who affected to be above those engaged in commercial pursuits, in the shape and size of their letters. But this letter, moreover, was sealed with wax, with a crest impressed on it, which the old Quaker viewed contemptuously; and his indignation was not soothed with the recollection that it was the device of the Milletts.

Lucy frequently received letters from her friends in the North, but they were unaccompanied with any superfluous show or expense. The wafer closed them, and the mark of the wafer stamp, making an impression like the punctures on a lady's thimble, was their only adornment.

This missive was immediately forwarded to the rightful owner, unaccompanied by any comment, or any desire of explanation.

Lucy expected that this letter would arrive, and she was pleased that it had been forwarded openly, and without any attempt at concealment; and it was the result that might follow that had cost so much sleepless anxiety,

She looked at it awhile as the omen of good or evil, and then, with trembling fingers, as ladies formerly were said to open the casket that contained their destiny, she opened the letter weighted with her fate.

She read as follows :—

"My DEAR MISS WESTON,—It is now more than three years ago that my father received a letter from Mr. Weston refusing his assent to an application for your hand which he made in my behalf; and having been informed that any correspondence that had not your father's approval would be distasteful to you, I have refrained from attempting it, although, if I might not hope for a nearer relationship, to have been blessed in my banishment with an epistle from you, would have been my greatest happiness.

"I have now returned after the completion of my services, which the Government have hought deserving of promotion, and they have raised me to the position of Commander.

"I mention these things in the hope that they will excuse the infringement of the condition imposed upon me, and, also, that you will suffer me—which I implore you not to prohibit—to apply, either personally or by letter, to Mr. Weston, asking his permission to see you.

"You have entreated me to forget you, and my reply is that I cannot. I have daily implored that Heaven would protect you, and so dispose the heart of your father that he might no longer place a barrier to the greatest happiness I ever hope to enjoy.

"If you still think me worthy of you, if you believe that the silent love of three long years is a proof of constant devotion, if you can trust, as I hope you can, that my whole life shall be spent in the promotion of your happiness, allow me, I beseech you, to ask your father for the greatest boon that earth can bestow.

"Waiting your reply with the deepest anxiety,

"I am, my dear Miss Weston,

"Your sincere and devoted

"GEORGE MILLETT."

Lucy's tears fell fast after reading the letter.

"This at least I will keep," said she to herself. "This will solace me in any event. His affection is like mine, it is a love for life. It shall be my pleasure and my pride to think of him; for to have the regard of so noble a man will compensate for all the trouble his love has occasioned."

She felt too excited by the reading of the letter to make any communication to her father on that day.

The good old Quaker, placid and mild, but more than usually grave, took his accustomed place at the tea-table, and passed the time without inquiry. He guessed that his daughter had received a letter from one of the Milletts, and Lucy believed that her father's anxious thoughts were on the contents of the letter.

He never feared that he should not be made acquainted with the object of it; but he apprehended—and the conversation with Rachel added to the conviction—that another application had been made.

The night following was passed by Lucy in restless apprehension. A little sleep crept over her after the old town clock had struck two in the morning, but it soon passed away, and left her alive to the anticipations of the coming day. Again she dozed in a half-dreaming, half-thinking condition, in which George Millett was ever present, but in so indistinct a character that the poor girl was

unable to decide whether she had been thinking or dreaming of him.

When the usual time arrived for attending
to the duties of the day, sleep overpowered her,
and when it was found that her place at the
breakfast-table was vacant, Rachel went to her
room to inquire the cause.

The opening of the door disturbed her, and
as the kind old domestic approached the bed
she saw the hectic flush that succeeds a sleepless
night.

" Thee art late to-day, Lucy, and I'm afraid
thee art not well. Thy father is waiting
breakfast. Shall I ask him not to wait?"

" Yes, please, Rachel. I've had a restless
night, and am now inclined to sleep. I will
remain in bed an hour or two. Ask my dear
father if he will please to excuse me."

" I will, my dear. Do thee go to sleep
again, and I'll take care that nothing shall
disturb thee."

CHAPTER VIII.

WHEN Jonathan Weston sat alone at the breakfast-table on the morning following the receipt
of the letter, he felt disappointed at the absence
of his daughter. It was a pleasant part of the
day—that breakfast-time.

The Quaker was himself a well-read man,
and it afforded him great pleasure to listen to
the observations of Lucy on the different subjects that, from time to time, were brought
under discussion.

The politics of the day were of a very exciting character.

The slave-trade was the utter abhorrence of
both, and only East India sugar—the produce
of free labour—was placed on the table. The
Test and Corporation Acts were duly criticized.
Catholic Emancipation had begun to be discussed, and on this subject they took opposite
sides—one represented the opinions that, like
himself, were dying out, and the other those
that were coming in. It was that time of great

public inquiry and discussion that preceded those momentous changes in the institutions of the country that have continued to the present time.

Mr. Weston had lived in the days of Pitt and Fox, Burke and Sheridan. They were now no more; but Canning, Plunket, Grey, Brougham, and Wilberforce were in the zenith of their glory.

Captivated by his eloquence, and admiring the broad and liberal views that he expounded, Lucy fought on the side of Canning; but her father, although liking him in general, disapproved of his Catholic proclivities. He revelled in the speeches of the young Robert Peel—the son of the Manchester manufacturer —which exhibited what he called the truly Protestant spirit. He did not live long enough to see those arguments refuted by the same Robert Peel, an older and a wiser man.

The conversations they had on those subjects that were uppermost in the world, and the keen encounter that sometimes occurred on those in which they held opposite opinions, were very agreeable to the old gentleman, and served to relieve the tedium of a rather monotonous life.

He missed at this morning meal his pleasant companion, and became concerned for her health.

"Hast thou offered, Rachel, to take anything to her?" said he. "Perhaps she would like a cup of coffee or tea."

"She won't have anything yet. She thinks she can sleep for an hour or two, and that's what the poor child wants."

Rachel here gave a very deep sigh, intended to be audible, at the same time placing her hands upon her hips, as if she required more than ordinary support.

"I saw that something was the matter," she continued, "before she went to bed last night. She said it was nothing; but she never makes anything of it, when it's herself that's ailing, bless her dear heart."

"How does she look, Rachel?"

"Looks like anybody else 'ell look that hasn't had a bit of sleep for the night—looks in a fever."

"Poor lamb! I will see her directly, and if she is feverish I will send for Doctor May."

"Don't thee go up. She said she would sleep a little, and after that come down. Neither Doctor May nor all the doctors in the world will do her any good. Her mind's disturbed, and I've never seen the physic that 'ell cure that."

Having delivered this last sentence in a rather spiteful tone, Rachel left the room, and, like a skilful orator, she allowed her master to ruminate on the most telling thing she had to say.

In silence and sorrow Jonathan Weston took his breakfast alone, believing that the letter, whatever might be its contents, had caused the depression which had been followed by a painful and sleepless night.

"When my daughter is more composed," thought he, "she will repose confidence in her father. I guess the purport of the missive. That Popish priest wishes his son to marry my daughter. What an alliance! The one the surpliced minister of ecclesiastical corruption, the other, bred a butcher, trades in blood. The Bengal tiger would mate with the gentle lamb, the vulture with the timorous dove! I must shield her from their fangs."

He rose from his seat and paced the room. It was difficult to be still while the mind was so busy. He walked to and fro in great perturbation, and after awhile sat down again.

The storm was abating. Another scene was passing before his mind. The Milletts were disappearing, and the pale and careworn features of Lucy Weston were gliding before his vision.

"I did not want Rachel to tell me of her pining grief and secret dejection," thought he. "I saw it! I saw it long ago! It worries me by day and disturbs me by night. What shall I say to her when she shows me the letter—as she will show it—and when she tells me that her hopes of life depend on my reply? Must I send her to the grave? Gentle, truthful, confiding, dutiful child, must I kill thee?"

Then again, his mind called forth another picture—the conclave of Friends. "Have I not urged upon them," said he to himself, "at all their meetings, uncompromising hostility to the priest and the man of blood? Have I not denounced them as the offspring of Satan, and the bland conductors to the bottomless pit? With what scorn will they tell me that I have married my daughter to the ministers of perdition! It cannot be; peace is departing from me, and a speedy grave is the most hopeful prospect of a man whose entanglements are more than he can bear."

In this vacillating mood reasoned the father —a benevolent, intelligent old gentleman, whose mind had received the highest cultivation of his sect, and who loved his only child with the fondness of one who believed her the greatest prize that man could possess.

His opinions, imbibed in childhood, strengthened with his growth, and had become confirmed by his association with the leaders of his sect.

The exclusion of Quakers from all posts of dignity, and from Parliament itself, rankled in the bosoms of that rich, proud, exclusive, and excluded people; while the peculiar tenets of their religion, their mode of worship—if worship it can be called—and their abhorrence of war, even when justified by oppression, or for the sake of defence, excluded the sympathy of other dissenters.

The sullen stubbornness of the sect had compelled an unwilling legislature to make their affirmation equivalent to an oath, and an alliance by civil contract a legal marriage. But the sufferings that wrung these compliances had embittered their feelings; and toleration had mitigated their penalties, but had left their ostility unsubdued.

The mind of Mr. Weston was disturbed by the mixed feelings of love for his daughter and hatred for the connexion she desired to form; and the view that might be taken of his compliance—if such a course could be possible—by the leaders of his association, added much to his perplexity.

Lucy was refreshed by the few hours' sleep, and, in the course of the morning, made her appearance in the parlour. Rachel, as she had been ordered, made the father acquainted with her arrival.

He immediately postponed the business he was engaged in, and went to see her.

"My love," said he on entering the room, and walking hastily towards her, kissing and embracing her with great tenderness, "I should have gone up to see thee, but Rachel said I had better not."

"Thank you, my dear father, I only needed a little rest. I am much better now; and when I have taken a little coffee, I will walk to Kellow beach."

"My dear lamb, thou art looking too weak for so long a walk. Shall I ask Dr. May to step in? I am concerned for thee; thy brow is hot, thy lips pale, and thy hands are moist. These are not the indications of health."

"No, thank you, father; I need repose more than anything else. I was much agitated yesterday, because" (her voice faltered and she hesitated), " because I had a favour to ask that I knew you were unwilling to grant. I wish you to see this" (she drew from her bosom the letter of George Millett), "and after you have carefully considered it, to give me your decision; and, if I might ask, in a matter in which the future of my life is concerned, I pray you to consider it favourably. I beseech you not to allow your prejudice against his profession to influence you; for, unless to serve his country, he would not injure a worm. He is not of our Society, but a more noble man does not exist. Three years ago you refused your assent; but a love like mine is not conquered by time—death only sees its conclusion. It is fed on hope as long as life lasts.

"I have obeyed you before, and I can do so again; but if the happiness of your daughter is of any concern to you, if—" Here the sobbing choked any further utterance, and the tears flowed over her pale face.

Her father trembled, and led her to the

sofa, and gently seating her, said, " I know what thou wouldst say, my child. I will consider the letter, and I will do all a father can for the happiness of one he loves so dearly. Do thou rest thyself and compose thy mind. I will read the letter, and let thee know."

He left her reclining on the sofa, and retired to his office. He read the letter, thought over it, and read it again. He placed it open upon his desk, and sat with his hand supporting his forehead. Having mused for a considerable time, he rose from the chair, and paced the room in perturbation and doubt. Now, his brow had a lowering aspect, and now again became serene.

At last he closed his lips firmly, and a stern resolution crept over his countenance. It was not his daughter's petition he was refusing, nor was he spurning the despised Millotts. He was defying some of the cold, hard, sneering, heartless men that he would have to meet in the conclave of his sect. He was denying that he was faithless to his creed, and defying the charge of revolt. He was asking them if he must kill his child ?

He waited till he became more composed,

that his resolve might seem the result of calm reflection.

Quakers do not subdue their passions—they disguise them; and few that behold the calm exterior suspect the fire that is burning within.

He returned to the parlour with the folded letter in his hand, which seemed to say, I want no further explanation of its contents.

He went up to his daughter, who was still reclining on the sofa, in the position he had left her. She was the picture of pale and almost hopeless resignation.

Overcome by the outburst of feeling that accompanied the presentation of the letter, a reaction of apathetic despondency succeeded, and that morbid indifference to external affairs that is the precursor of decline, disease, and death.

Without at first speaking a word, Mr. Weston kissed and embraced his daughter. He saw to what a state of utter hopelessness her former excitement and his delay had reduced her, and he felt nerved to pursue the course he had determined to adopt.

"My love," said he, "have a little con-- fidence in thy father. Things are not always so gloomy as they seem. I am bound to tell thee that I like the strong affection and sound sense of this letter."

At this intelligence Lucy sat upright, and looked into his countenance with a supplicating smile.

" It is different," he continued, " from what I expected, and has none of that maudlin sentimentality that is so offensive. If it be so much the desire of thy heart to wed this man, I will consult the Friends on the subject."

The hope that was beaming on Lucy's countenance disappeared. She knew the Friends; and if it depended on their concurrence, she could never be George Millett's bride. Mr. Weston saw the change, and proceeded to explain.

" They have a right to expect this. That Jonathan Weston should hand over his daughter to a man of Belial——"

A frown clouded Lucy's brow, and a flush of indignation inflamed her countenance; and she was about to repel the unjust aspersion.

" Don't be displeased, my child; I am speaking as they will reason. They will say that I am false to my faith, and a deserter of my church !"

" Then, my dear father, let the penalty of

my unfortunate attachment fall upon the head
that deserves it. Did you think that I could
be happy in a position that had brought down
disgrace upon the grey hairs of my father?"

"I will not take advantage, my love, of thy
affection, any more than I will suffer the
Friends to judge the motives that actuate my
own breast. To seem to be a deserter of my
church is one thing; to be the thing that my
reason condemns is another. I have not so
learnt the principles that George Fox incul-
cated as to guide my conduct in accordance
with the opinions of other people. As I shall
pay them a poor compliment to ask their
advice after I have given my consent, I must
ask thee to defer any positive answer to the
young man until I give thee permission. At
the same time, my darling" (and he looked
lovingly on her as he said it), "I shall not feel
bound to abide by *their* advice."

At hearing this, Lucy rose from the sofa,
and, placing her arms around the old patri-
arch's neck, kissed him again and again,
exclaiming, "O, my love of a father!"

The old man continued,—"Thou mayst
reply to George Millett, that if he thinks it
worth his while to wait for a definite answer,

it will be forwarded to him when I have fully decided. In the mean time, with his reply to thy letter, which he may think it necessary to make, I must ask thee to let the position remain on the same terms as before."

"He will wait, my dear father, and he will bless you, even for this; and he will bless you for more, for I feel it cannot be but that we shall be united."

Thus had the revolution of one day affected the prospects of two persons, who valued above the riches and splendours of the world the permission to pass their pilgrimage together.

But what might the convocation of saints produce? Might they not again steel the heart of the benevolent Quaker? If there was much for congratulation, there was also much for apprehension. How true, that the sweetest cup has its bitter ingredient, and every rose a thorn.

CHAPTER IX.

ON the day following the interview related in the last chapter, between Mr. Weston and his daughter, Lucy sat down to write to George Millett. It was only now, when she had taken a restrospect of what had occurred, and when she had to set down in plain words the result, that she felt how little she had gained.

Previously she had an indefinable impression that the outworks of the citadel were stormed, and that from this additional vantage-ground the other impediments must yield. Perhaps this was the true position of affairs; but what had her father empowered her to write? Was it that the Captain's offer had been accepted, but that he wished the fulfilment of it to be postponed? She wished she could say so. She had a feeling that something of that kind was meant; but she must be frank with George Millett, honest to herself, and just to her father.

She must not delude George with hopes

that might not be realized—she must not, on her own account, set down impressions for promises — and must not twist her father's words to a meaning they did not fairly bear. She therefore wrote to him the following letter.

" Dear Captain Millett, — Allow me in the first place to congratulate you on your promotion, and on your safe return from your long voyage. I received your very, *very* kind letter, and I thank you from my heart for the many kind things you have written, and for your daily remembrance of me through the long and tedious years that have passed since our last meeting. I do not wish to conceal from you that I also have daily offered up my prayers for your safe and happy return, although I had no right to hope that you would return to me.

"I have laid your letter before my father, with my earnest entreaty that he would allow me to give you a favourable reply. I sat down to write under the conviction that his love for his daughter had conquered his hostility to your profession; but since I began, I have had a misgiving that his words will not bear so favourable an interpretation.

" I wish to be open and plain with you, and honest to my father. His words were to this effect.

" 'If George Millett thinks it worth his while to wait for a definite answer, it can be forwarded to him when I have fully decided. In the mean time, with his reply to thy letter —which he may think it necessary to make— I must ask that your position to each other remain on the same terms as before.'

" I have no right to expect, with such an answer, that you will wait any longer for me. Go—and Heaven bless you—where you will be more worthily received. You have suffered humiliation enough on my account. I thank you that your affection has enabled you to bear it. I shall regret that our creeds have separated us. but shall not cease to pray for your welfare.

" Your faithful friend,
" Lucy Weston."

This letter duly reached its destination, and if any reader supposed that it would drive George Millett to the antipodes, it was a great mistake. On the contrary, his delight was beyond bounds. He looked upon it as if the enemy had hauled

VOL. II.   I

down his flag. If the Quaker had been in his immediate vicinity, he would have embraced him, although the shock of such an impropriety would probably have caused a reaction.

He sufficiently moderated his enthusiasm as to be able to write; but as love-letters are very uninteresting, except to those personally affected, we will omit this particular effusion, and only remark that it began with, "My dearest, *dearest* Lucy," and so far differed from his former effort, that if her father had seen this instead of the other, he would not have characterized it as an epistle of good sense and sobriety. He proceeded to say that he would wait till eternity, which was a longer time than any charitable person would wish. Strange to relate, prudent and sensible as Lucy was, she preferred this wild effusion to the former, saying, " It was more like George."

Things had now progressed—not quite so well as the lovers might desire—much better than their former prospects had warranted them to expect. Their correspondence ceased, and Lucy's health and spirits revived.

One day, when the agitation of these proceedings had subsided, and Lucy's mind had again settled into its usual composure, she sat on the old-fashioned window-seat of her father's house, busily engaged on her embroidery. Her imagination was painting beautiful pictures, totally unconnected with the flowers that were growing under the guidance of her busy fingers. The streets were noiseless in that little old-fashioned town, where passers-by could be both seen and heard.

Soon there was a sudden commotion. People were running by in haste, and street doors were opened for the purpose of asking what was the matter.

A sailor ran, almost breathless, down the street, and told them, while he continued his speed, that the smugglers and coast-guard were fighting in the bay.

This extraordinary news drew forth the inmates from every house, and no one felt more concerned than Lucy Weston herself.

She rang the bell, and soon the trusty Rachel appeared.

"A man has gone by," said Lucy, "saying that the smugglers and officers are fighting at sea. Wilt thou kindly go to the hill, and inquire into the truth of it?"

Rachel always preferred to be addressed in the Quaker's idiom, especially by her young mistress, both because she thought it more Christian-like, and because she herself had taught that language to Lucy in her infantine years.

"Yes, my dear, I will go," said Rachel, but at the same time she sighed a sigh.

"I know," said Lucy, who guessed that the labour of such a journey was the cause of the distress, "I know that it is difficult for thee to get up the hill; but I am afraid if thou sendst the girl, she will bring back some Banbury story that nobody will understand."

"Yes, Banbury enough when it com'th," said Rachel, "and, bad as 'twill be, 'twill be a long time a-coming. 'Tisn't as it used to be when I was young. If that maid mits with Sam Lewis by the way, if she gits back before night 'tis a wonder."

Lucy herself sighed at hearing this, and thought if Sam Lewis had been Rachel's lover, she would not have thought a little delay so criminal.

"Perhaps we may as well wait till the news comes to us," she said.

"No, my dear," said Rachel; "I shall go myself; though I'm that stout that I shall pant a good many times before I git to the top. Once I was as thin as a lath, as people say."

Lucy smiled, and said, "I think that was a long time ago."

"Yes; before I used to take thee by thy two arms, and taich thee to put one foot before the other. But I shall git to the top of the hill after a while, for I dare say thou wishest to know if Edith Phinn's husband is in the fray, as is likely enough. How that girl kum to marry that man I can't think. He's allis a-gittin' into some scrummage. If any man comes a-courtin' to me, and goes a-drowning of hisself to show his love, he shall go to the bottom of the say before I'll jump after 'n."

Lucy had hitherto preserved a sedate countenance, but this was irresistible, and she laughed in the face of her old nurse, because it was inconceivable that any man could be so smitten with Rachel's charms as to drown himself on her account, and equally impossible, with her ponderous weight, that she could leap to the rescue.

"Thou shalt never be married with my consent," she said. "I cannot do without thee; so I must beg thee not to give any man encouragement."

"I kips 'em at a distance, my dear, and they don't come to me a second time tellin' their love."

She said this with great gravity, nodding her head in token of her determination, and then left the room with an air of conscious merit. Rachel, during her long service, had acquired a little property, and it was whispered that two or three needy neighbours had aspired to her hand.

She divested herself of her checked apron, and started off in her brown stuff dress, surmounted by a black silk Quaker's bonnet of the most orthodox coal-scuttle shape.

She was one of the characters of the place, and her position in her master's house was not only very peculiar, but she was also a person of importance in public estimation. The highest and richest had a kind word for her, and the poor regarded her as adviser and friend. Some of them, too needy to afford the medical advice they required, attended to the suggestions and recommendations of this experienced practitioner; and many a family had passed through the numerous ills that childhood is heir to under the healing appliances of this benevolent old woman.

When she had surmounted the hill, her inquiries were immediately attended to by an old naval captain, who had served with credit in the late war, and was now resting on his laurels and his half-pay in this secluded little seaport. Although few naval officers go to sea for pleasure, probably impressed by past experience that its prospects are delusive, none of them prefer a residence in an inland town.

In this place, in consequence of the withdrawal of so many ships from active service, their number was large; and they might be distinguished on the sea-side by their spy-glass and their peculiar gait. They would go about twenty yards with a short quick step, and then stop with a sudden jerk, as if the barrier of the quarter-deck had intercepted their progress, and, turning to the "right-about face," would pace over again their measured walk.

It was one of those old veterans that supplied Rachel with the information required.

"One man is shot," said he, "and the boats are returning to port; but, if the calm continues, a gun-boat from Plymouth will give a good account of that black flag."

Rachel's sympathies were on the other side.

She had often accompanied Lucy to the island, and, although she disapproved of Edith's marriage with so reckless a man, she felt an interest in the fate of Lascare on Edith's account.

While she was looking on, the soft, but friendly, breeze sprang up, the lofty sails of the light craft immediately felt its influence, and she glided from her dangerous position with miraculous speed. The bystanders looked at each other in wonder, for the burdened coasters were but little affected by the light wind.

"Stole away, by Jove!" said an old tar, delighted that the Government was beaten.

"Now, then," said Rachel, radiant with pleasure as she saw the Swift glide out of the bay; "now, then, the smuggler has escaped."

"I tell you, Rachel," said the Captain, with asperity, displeased at such an exhibition of feeling against constituted authority, "some man has committed an act to-day that he will not be allowed long to repent of."

These ominous words were conveyed back to Lucy, and again, in the old Quaker's establishment, the sunshine was succeeded by gloom.

"Did they say it was Lascare's vessel?" asked Lucy.

"Captain Williams told me," replied Rachel, "that the Government had sent a description of Lascare's sloop to the chief officer, and that the hull and rig of that in the bay answered to the description, and that the smugglers called her the Swift."

"I am afraid," said Mr. Weston, "that Edith's husband has made his last voyage, and that he will relinquish his calling as much from compulsion as design."

"Do you think, father, they will take him?"

"He may escape; but I wish he may be wise enough not to visit his native land again."

"What will poor Edith do?" said Lucy. "Her life is devoted to the man. She will seek him to the world's end."

While this conversation was taking place Lascare was making all sail from the coast, and by sun-set had arrived at the middle of the Channel. Here he called his crew together, and made them acquainted with the plan of his future proceedings.

"I shall sail," said he, "for Nantes, and trust no more to Crosaix. That loafer we saw every day lounging on the quay has brought this trouble upon us. At Nantes there is a merchant in the salt trade, called Menier, that our people at home always deal with. He is a very respectable man, and I will ask him to write to John Spillar. It won't do for us to write, because the Government will find us out, and set spies upon us. Our comrades at home will know best what should be done, and we will wait for an answer from them. Now I don't regret the stand we made, but I'm sorry for the poor fellow that's shot. It would have been more serious work if they had all come on. You stood by me like men. If they recommend throwing up the trade, I will see that all your expenses on your journey home shall be paid. We've got richer men to back us than the world knows of."

The crew agreed that the course he intended to pursue was, under the circumstances, the best.

The excitement of the fray had now subsided, and a misgiving as to the consequence had succeeded. They could not penetrate the dusky cloud lowering in the future. Pride, anger, cupidity, and defiance had urged them on, but now their minds were embittered by success. Nevertheless, they bore up against their fate like brave and resolute men, and they agreed that, come what might, they would stand by each other.

"Let no man of us," said Edward Allen, the mate, "breathe a word of what orders we had, or who fired. If they had come on, we should all have fired. But my mind tells me that the smugglin' trade's over, and we shall know better what to be at when we hear from Tregarth."

The propitious east wind that wafted them from the bay carried them with flowing sail from the English Channel, and, passing the island of Ushant, they felt relieved from the apprehension of danger, for there was no doubt that the revenue cutters had orders for their capture. They passed Ushant in the night, keeping due south, and, nearing the land at daylight, they opened the French coast.

Scudding by the fatal Crosaix, as if an ambush lay there, they felt they had abandoned a long-frequented course that would see them no more.

Before the next night they entered the Loire, and on the following day sailed up the harbour of Nantes, and lay at last, with a feeling of security, by the quay of a friendly port.

On their arrival, Lascare sought the French merchant, and explained to him their perilous position.

He had taken the liberty, he said, to ask his advice and assistance, because some of the owners of the cruiser were customers of his, and he knew that Mr. Zechariah Drew, the banker, of Tregarth, who sent him the remittances for salt, would feel deeply obliged for any assistance he could render.

Nothing could have been more fortunate than Lascare's application to the French merchant. His frequent exportations to the Cornish and Devonshire ports had made him acquainted with the names of many persons who resided on the coast, and had obtained for him a smattering knowledge of the English language; but what, in the present instance, was of the greatest value, was that his son was a resident in Cornwall, who had been sent to that locality for the twofold purpose of acquiring a knowledge of the English language, and of making himself acquainted with the correspondents of his father.

The history of the perilous cruise of the Swift enlisted the sympathies of the French merchant, who immediately supplied the captain with money for his present wants, and offered his services in the promotion of any scheme his owners might direct.

He forwarded a letter from Lascare to John Spillar, enclosed to his son, and urged on the latter the necessity that those communications should be secret. He also requested him to place himself in communication with Spillar, and to report to him what course it was intended to pursue when the owners of the cargo had arrived at a definite conclusion.

CHAPTER X.

Four weeks passed away after the Swift had
entered the harbour of Nantes, and no reply
had been received from Tregarth. M. Menier
did all he could devise to relieve the drooping
spirits of the crew. He sent presents to the
seamen, and invited the captain to his house.
His family also, with the generous warmth of
that impulsive nation, endeavoured to divert
the mind of Lascare from brooding over the
fatal shot, and the sad desolation of his wife.

He was made one of the family circle, and,
in return for their kindness, he related to his
new acquaintance his past adventures, his
many fights, his perils on the sea, and, last of
all, the danger from which his heroic wife had
saved him. His knowledge of the French
language, which he had acquired by his frequent visits to Crosaix, was now of great service to him.

The daring man became a great favourite
with his friendly host, who made him feel as

little as possible the painful position in which he was placed. At length the expected letter arrived from young Menier, with an enclosure from Spillar to Lascare.

The young student had been equal to the occasion. He placed no trust in the officials of the post-office, and made a journey to Tregarth, professedly for the purpose of visiting his father's customers; but he took the opportunity of placing Lascare's letter into the hands of the surprised John Spillar.

He led the old veteran apart from the others, under the pretence of inquiring into their method of curing the fish; and, drawing from his pocket the entrusted enclosure, held up the writing of Lascare, to the astonishment of his companion.

The cautious manner in which it was conveyed warned Spillar that secrecy was important; and having concealed it about his person, they again joined the rest of the company.

Spillar now pretended that he must attend to another engagement, and requesting the young Frenchman to call at his house before he took his departure—the object of which was understood—he proceeded to consult the chiefs of the co-partnership, and by the time that M. Menier called the reply was ready.

Great anxiety and alarm prevailed at Tregarth after the departure of the Swift, and the continued absence of all information respecting her added mystery to the apprehension. It was therefore soothing to 'the connexions of the crew to know that their relatives were safe; but the means by which that knowledge had been obtained, as well as the place of their retreat, were not disclosed.

By the letter, conveyed by the son of M. Menier, the captain was informed that at a meeting of the owners it had been decided that the Swift and cargo should be sold, and the crew provided, in addition to their wages, with sufficient money for their journey home; but there was a strong recommendation that, on their arrival in England, they should return singly, and make their appearance after dark. This was particularly urged, because warrants had been issued for the apprehension of the crew.

In about a week after the reception of this letter, the Swift and cargo were sold; the French merchant was reimbursed for his outlay; and Lascare, after taking a grateful farewell of his entertainers, started for Calais with his crew.

On their arrival he sent off the seamen singly, day after day, and at the end of a week started himself for Dover, with a heavier heart than he ever before carried to his native shore.

It added to his distress, that neither Edith nor any of his friends dared to address a letter to him; and what might be the watch for him at Tregarth, or what might be the safest route, were matters of great perplexity. One thing he determined on—come what might, he would see his wife.

On his arrival at Dover, he conceived it might be dangerous to take the usual route to Cornwall; he therefore proceeded in the first place to London, and remained in the city until the afternoon of the following day. At four o'clock the next day the stage-coach started from the Bull and Mouth, with a few persons on the outside, and Lascare and a Quaker gentleman on the inside. He preferred to travel in as private a manner as possible, as he had no doubt his personal appearance was fully described in the *Hue and Cry*, a paper that was issued by the Government for the purpose of giving information of the distinctive characteristics of the individuals they desired to ensnare.

Lascare was by no means a loquacious person; and the taciturnity of Quakers on a journey is systematic, it being their rule of conduct to say as little as possible before strangers, unless an opportunity of exhortation or reproof should arise. Therefore, from the Bull and Mouth, in St. Martin's-le-Grand, to the White Horse Cellars, in Piccadilly, not a word was spoken by either.

The Quaker had an umbrella in his hand, which was carefully protected by a green cotton case; and there was carved on the ivory handle the name of Samuel Cleave, Bristol.

At the White Horse was waiting for the coach a bustling and rather boisterous gentleman, who had sundry packages covered with black leather, which he directed to be placed in the fore boot. All this being duly accomplished, the guard opened the door of the coach, and a commercial gent, as he was called, swung himself in, saying, "Good evening, gentlemen," to the previous occupants, and seating himself opposite to the Quaker.

Lascare did not care to be observed, and lay

back in his own corner, without appearing to notice the new arrival.

The guard sounded his horn, and the four prancing horses started for the first stage.

When they were fairly off, the new comer scrutinized his companions, and having taken stock of them, turned his head to the window with a grunt.

It was evident to him that he had travelled in more agreeable company.

Not daunted, however, by the inanimate sobriety of the Friend, he opened with,— " We 've had a pleasant day, sir."

" The weather has been agreeable," was the reply.

For some time no further conversation ensued. After a little cogitation, he again came to the fore. " Splendid season for trade."

" Ah ! " said the Quaker.

The discomfited commercial reclined his rather extensive person on the side of the coach, and ruminated there for two or three hours, having passed over a few stages in the mean time.

The coach was now brought to a stand, and the guard, opening the door, announced that they would stop there half-an-hour.

The gentleman descended, and left the Quaker and Lascare behind. It was evident that they either did not want refreshments, or declined to make their appearance.

At the tea-table the bustling traveller was joined by others from the outside seats, and he informed them that he had "two of the queerest devils on the inside that it had ever been his misfortune to travel with."

"What sort of fellows are they?" inquired one of the passengers.

"One of them is a Quaker, and he has summoned up a sufficient amount of articulation as to say, 'Ah!' The other is a Frenchman, as I think, for he has not only not spoken a word, but I have not yet seen the whole of his countenance, though I have not been backward in taking advantage of every opportunity."

"Why," said the other, "didn't you try a bit of French?"

"I did. When the leader began to plunge, I swore in French. It was the only bit of learning I could command for the moment; but even the sound of his own mother-tongue didn't elicit a word."

The guard sounded his horn, and the pas-

sengers took their seats. It was now dark,
but the glare of the lamps showed a figure
in the corner, as the commercial gentleman
entered the coach.

"How are you now, sir?" said he, addressing Mr. Cleave.

"Thank thee, friend, I am tolerably well,"
was the reply, and the conversation ended.

A few stages further on, the restless gentleman again got out "to wet his whistle,"
as he said. On re-entering the coach, he again
called out,—"Well, sir, how are you now?"

"I am pretty well, thank thee," was the
reply, and again solemn silence reigned.

The Quaker now hung up his broad-brim,
and mounted his nightcap, and applied himself to repose. Once more the coach pulled
up for supper, and the active traveller again
descended, to take in his last support for the
night.

All being now still, Mr. Cleave was enjoying
a sound sleep, while the commercial was wash-
ing down a good supper with strong spirits.
After the usual time had elapsed, he again
returned, and in a tone louder than before,
said,—"How are you now, sir?"

Startled from sleep by this unnecessary inquiry, the indignant Quaker replied,—"I am just the same, friend, as when thou asked me last; and if any change occurs, I will let thee know."

The night passed by, and the cold, grey morning came in; and after a few more stages, the coach brought up at the Feathers, in the time-honoured capital of the west.

The Plume of Feathers was, even at that time, an interesting remnant of ancient days. It was a quadrangular building, including a square courtyard, which was entered from the street through an arch. It seems to have been the favourite design for inns previous to the Elizabethan age; but very few at the present time remain. There was one in the Borough of Southwark some few years since, and there is one at Gloucester, which still retains its ancient reputation, and was a resting-place of Queen Elizabeth in her tour through the country. The present architecture for hotels, as they are now called, is neither so picturesque nor convenient; although the economy of space, which in large towns is very important, is superior.

The quadrangle was bordered on all sides by a corridor, and through that was the passage to the sleeping apartments, which were entered from it. The only inconvenience being—which formerly was not thought important—that the passage from the sitting-room to the bed-room was exposed to the open air, although it was protected by a roof.

The coach entered the courtyard, the reins were thrown to the grooms, and the passengers proceeded to dismount. The Quaker and the commercial gentleman descended from the coach, and went immediately to look after their luggage, the one keeping his eye to the top of the coach, the other to the fore-boot.

While all were thus busily engaged, Lascare took up his carpet bag, which he had taken with him into the inside, and stepping into the yard, slipped through the arch, and mixed, unobserved, with the people in the street.

He had been in Bristol before, and he took his way to an inn that was well known to him, frequented by masters of vessels; feeling more confident of his security among persons of his own class than with a people to whom his appearance might seem peculiar.

His object at first was to continue his journey to Cornwall, through the north of Devon, and to avoid Exeter and Plymouth.

But the more he reflected on his precarious situation, and the probable espionage that surrounded his home, the more he became inclined to delay his appearance, for he wisely conceived that his chance of meeting his wife with security would be improved by allowing time for the evaporation of the enemy's zeal.

It also occurred to him that he would be more secure in a large city, where he could pass unknown and unobserved, and where he might also devise means for communicating with his friends without fear of detection.

It was now that the kindness of Mr. Weston and his daughter presented itself; and although he had no personal knowledge of them, he felt than he need not hesitate to enlist their services, for the kind-hearted Edith had given him glowing accounts of the favours bestowed on her, before he had made the acquaintance of the pretty island maid.

He conceived the plan of causing a letter to be forwarded under cover to Mr. Weston, by one of the Quaker merchants of Bristol; and that Edith's reply would reach him, if his project should be successful, through Mr. Weston, and under cover to the Bristol merchant.

By this means there would be no knowledge

that any correspondence had taken place; and
there would be no necessity that he should
confine himself to one locality, or that he should
create suspicion by attendance at the post-
office.

He knew no one of Bristol that would be
likely to assist him, and his mind reverted to
the sober visage of his late fellow-traveller by
the stage coach. Samuel Cleave was engraven
on the handle of the umbrella; and as there
was nothing else to designate his abode, it was
an indication of a frugal, well-known, and
opulent man.

He applied to his landlord for information,
and discovered that Mr. Cleave was a rich tea-
dealer of the city, and that his office was not
very distant. On the third day after his
arrival, he determined to ask the assistance of
Mr. Cleave, and went forthwith to the merchant's office. He rang the bell. An elderly
man, dressed in drab coat and breeches, with
light grey hose, and large buckles in his shoes,
opened the door, and said,—

"What dost thou want, friend?"

"I wish to see Mr. Cleave," said Lascare,
"if he is disengaged and can attend to me for
a few minutes."

" Samuel Cleave is always engaged, friend,
when he is at this office.   Is thy business of a
nature that it requires secrecy?"

"It does."

"Then what name shall I call thee, if I may
not know thy business?"

"You will please to say to Mr. Cleave that
a person in distress seeks his assistance."

"Samuel Cleave dispenses his charities at
his private residence, friend; and if thy business is of so private a nature that it cannot be
disclosed, thou hadst better seek him at a time
when he is occupied with affairs of less importance."

Lascare was not inclined to make any reve-
lations to so inquisitive a person, and felt
indignant at the insinuation that he sought
pecuniary relief. "I called to see Mr. Cleave,"
said he, "in the hope that he would communicate with a gentleman of his own position, and
relate the message that I shall give him.   The
advantage of this service will be mine, and he
will receive thanks for his kindness from a
higher quarter; but if Mr. Cleave keeps you
at the entrance of his office to prevent an interview with any person that does not bring him
profit, or if your curiosity must first be satisfied

before admittance can be granted, he is not
the kind of gentleman I called here to see."

In saying this he looked at the man in drab
with withering scorn.

The officious clerk was surprised and frightened at the spirit of this reply, and he began
at once to soothe the irritation his prying,
disposition had provoked, and he became
as obsequious as he had been before offensive.

"Wilt thou please to take a seat," said he.
"I will make Samuel Cleave acquainted with
thy presence immediately the person he is
engaged with has left his private room. Thou
art a stranger to Bristol, I see; thy speech
betrays thee. Thou hast had fine weather for
travelling; or—I beg thy pardon" (here he
smiled, and bowed at a supposed mistake)—
"for sailing."

"Yes," said Lascare, looking with contempt
at the supple and crawling thing before him,
"yes, the *weather* is fine enough."

Just as this was said, the door of the inside
apartment opened, and a gentleman walked
out. Immediately the clerk went in, and,
returning after a few minutes' absence, informed Lascare that "Samuel Cleave waited
to see him."

As Lascare entered the *sanctum sanctorum* of the Bristol merchant, he saw before him, seated at the further end of the table, his former companion in the stage-coach. He was a tall, thin man. His face was pale rather than fair, and the crown of his head was perfectly bald. Lascare felt, on entering, that he was scrutinized from head to foot. The Quaker motioned to him to take a seat, and, as the sailor did so, the small, keen eye of the Friend explored the whole contour of his visage.

"Have I seen thy face before?"

"Yes, sir, the other day in a journey from London."

"I am informed that thou hast some private communication to make to me."

"I have not," said Lascare, "but I have a favour to ask. I have no apology to make for intruding upon you, except that I am a stranger and in distress."

"That is a sufficient apology to a Christian man. What dost thou want?"

"In the first place, sir, I wish to know if you are acquainted with Mr. Weston, the banker of Penwith, in Cornwall."

"I have a slight knowledge of him, but he is no particular acquaintance of mine. I have met him at some of our annual meetings. But why didst thou ask?"

"Because Mr. Weston is a friend to my wife; and I beg of you the favour of sending her this letter, enclosed to him."

"The favour is a very trifling one, my friend, which I will not refuse thee; but excuse my asking, as the Post-Office is open to all, why thou canst not do it for thyself?"

As Mr. Cleave said this, he watched carefully the effect of his question on the countenance of the stranger, and perceived that he had touched the chord to which his feelings were most sensitive.

Lascare now felt that if he enlisted the interest of a stranger in his affairs, he must be prepared to reward it with confidence. It was now his turn to investigate character. There was a mild benevolence in the features of Mr. Cleave, combined with an appearance of keen intellect and sound sense. He would trust him, he thought.

"Mr. Cleave," said he, "the bloodhounds are watching for my trail. I care not to live to be banished from my wife. More than this it will do you no good to know, and might do harm."

"Enough, my friend," said the Quaker. "Thou shalt have all the service I can render thee; and I will write to Jonathan Weston that he may enclose to me thy wife's reply. It is very true that there is a great deal of knowledge that we are nothing the better for, and, as thou art disinclined to be communicative, I will not press thee."

"I thought, sir, that you might be inclined to do a charitable deed for an unhappy man without asking why it was required, and it may be that you would regret the knowledge when you had it."

"I am pleased to find," said Mr. Cleave, "that thou art capable of keeping thy own counsel; one half of the evils of the world are created by excessive talk. I will forward thy letter forthwith, and thou mayst come for the answer when thou thinkst it may be likely to arrive."

The benevolent Quaker then shook hands with the unknown sailor, and bade him farewell.

CHAPTER XI.

THREE days after the conversation between Lascare and Mr. Cleave, the post brought among other letters to the bank of Mr. Weston one to the following effect:—

" Jonathan Weston, Penwith.

"Bristol, 20th of 11 mo. 1821.

"RESPECTED FRIEND,—A person of whom I have no knowledge, having the appearance of a master of a vessel, of more than ordinary intelligence, and of a marked character, hath requested me to forward the enclosed letter to thee. I have promised him, in case thou shouldst enclose a reply to myself, to let him have it.

"I fear the man is in some trouble, and I found him rather uncommunicative; but if it be a matter of charity to serve him, I shall have no objection to place my services at thy disposal.

"I remain,

"Thy friend sincerely,

"SAMUEL CLEAVE."

After the perusal of the foregoing letter, Jonathan Weston carried it to his daughter, and they both immediately understood why that mode of conveyance had been adopted.

"My dear father," said Lucy, "if you will hire a boat to take me to Tregarth, I will carry the letter to Edith, and bring back the answer to it. This is the hardest fate of all. They dare not meet."

"Thou shalt, my dear child, and give my love to her, and say, if I can be of any service, she must not hesitate to employ me."

Within one hour from the receipt of the letter, Lucy Weston was on her voyage to Tregarth, carrying the only remedy that, for the present, could relieve the afflicted mind of Edith Lascare.

On the afternoon of that day she was sitting in her little room, which we can hardly dignify with the name parlour; yet it deserved the name, if neatness and good arrangement entitled it to the appellation, for it was ornamented, in addition to the fire-arms and weapons of war that struck the attention of Lucy on a former visit, with sundry antique pieces of china, pictures of the battle of the Nile and of Trafalgar, of the funeral of Lord

Nelson, rather gorgeously painted for such a solemn ceremonial, and sundry other pictures of smaller dimensions.

There were also on the mantel-piece profiles of Lascare and his wife covered with glass and ornamented with ebony frames; and there were shells of various kinds and sizes, that once occupied the shoals of foreign seas.

Edith was sitting in this retiring-room—whatever may be its proper name—knitting, busily at times, and again stopping to listen to some ·further revelation from an acquaintance, who was engaged in the twofold occupation of knitting a Guernsey frock for her husband and relating the adventures of the last voyage of the Swift.

This other person was the wife of Edward Allen, the mate of that ill-fated cruiser. Her husband was the last of the crew that arrived at Tregarth, who, with the advice of his friends, had caused it to be reported that he had again left the neighbourhood, although, in reality, he was concealed at his own home.

The chief adventures of this last voyage had been heard before; but as Mary Allen could give a more particular account, she was, at the present time, the most desirable companion; for Edith's mind was entirely absorbed in her anxieties for the fate of her husband—at one time wishing to see him—at another, in the hope that he was far, far away.

The conversation was interrupted by the arrival of Lucy Weston, at which Edith's friend considerately withdrew.

Her relatives dead, and Lascare roaming the country in disguise—whose fireside was the most dangerous place in the wide world— Edith's mind reverted again and again to Lucy as her only support; and at that moment her constant friend stood before her.

Lucy kissed her with all the warmth of their earliest love, and asked if she knew anything of the movements of her husband.

"Nothing," said Edith, "but that he was left alone at Calais."

"Then you would be glad to know, if any one could only tell you where he is?"

"Delighted, and to know that he is safe."

"Then I can tell you that he is safe, and at Bristol!"

"Thank you, thank you, my dear Lucy; but how do you know?"

"I will produce my evidence," said Lucy,

taking out the letter, and showing his own handwriting.

Smiles and tears came together as Edith broke the wax impressed with Richard's own seal!

Edith read the familiar writing, at first with rapidity, and afterwards read it over again more slowly, and coming to the end she sighed heavily.

"I hope I have brought you no evil tidings?" said Lucy.

"No, no! Before you came I thought I could be contented with such a letter as this—to know that he is safe, and where; but now it is come, I want a great deal more—I want to see him."

She was about to proceed, but the tears filled her eyes, and she could say no more. After a while she recovered.

"Don't think me ungrateful—I shall never forget your kindness; but how long can anything give me pleasure while Richard dares not come to his home?

"He tells me that I must send my reply through Mr. Weston, and I am sure you will take it; but I must first see some of his friends. Oh! how good you are! Might I ask you to remain here alone while I seek their advice?

They are all very kind to me. Mr. Drew, the banker, comes to see me every day, and if money could buy it, we might again live in peace. I shall not be long. I will give the letter to John Spillar, who will consult the others, and he will bring me their decision."

"My dear Edith, do not go in such a hurry. Compose yourself. I can wait, even if your friends take till midnight to consult. I have two powerful men to take me back."

Edith sat down for a few minutes, during which time she endeavoured to show that she had mastered her agitation and become composed. She then left to show the letter to her friends.

In less than ten minutes she returned, and informed Lucy that John Spillar would see the other adventurers, and bring the result of their conference.

In the mean time Edith made tea, and all being duly served, these two old friends sat at the tea-table together. It then occurred to Lucy how often, in the happy days of childhood, they had played at making tea, when limpet-shells served for cups and a skerry-shell for a tea-pot. Since then, the old people had passed away, and they themselves had entered on the real duties of life. Other affections had grown up—different desires and different tastes—and the delights of former years pleased them no more.

But they were succeeded by other happy faces, who revelled in their imaginary occupations on the beach.

Edith felt relieved in the companionship of her old friend, and hoped that through Mr. Weston she should have frequent correspondence with her husband.

Soon after the tea was laid aside, a tall, elderly man presented himself, who was introduced to Miss Weston as John Spillar.

He was remarkably erect for his age, of good form, and muscular limbs. His head was bald, and the scanty locks that still lingered by the side were approaching to white. His forehead was not broad, but high, and his eyes were small and piercing. His complexion was dark, but singularly bright and clear, and the expression of his countenance was remarkably mild.

He was dressed in a blue cloth suit, but the material was of superior quality, and the jacket rather longer than those of the present day.

His scholastic education had been very meagre, but he had supplemented it by his intercourse with different classes of society, and his intellect was naturally keen and observant. He was courteous and respectful, without any pretension to gentility, firm and resolute without passion, and, never seeming to demand it, the chief place at the council board became his by natural right. This was the leading chieftain of Tregarth, a man bold to project, and cautious to execute.

This ancient mariner, who had been an early adventurer in the privateer, and had acquired a considerable fortune, was connected from first to last [with the history we have attempted to relate. He was the foster-father of Lascare, and the medium of communication between the smugglers and Zechariah Drew.

As soon as Edith had introduced him, he addressed himself to Lucy.

"The people of Tregarth will feel deeply obliged to you, Miss Weston, and to your excellent father, when the time comes that they should know what good service you have done them. At present it will be necessary for us to keep the matter secret, that we may have further advantage of the correspondence. We have decided that Edith should desire her husband to remain at Bristol, and I am re-

quested to ask that Mr. Weston will be kind
enough to allow her letters to be sent through
him. The Government will use the Post-Office
to discover our designs, but by this method
they will hardly succeed. And now, my dear,"
said he, addressing Edith as his daughter,
"tell Dick we intend to let the storm blow
over, and when we think it will be safe to
come home we will let him know. Don't forget
to say that all send their kind remembrances,
and that nothing that can be done will be left
untried. Good-bye, Miss Weston; and I hope
you will have as pleasant a voyage to Penwith
as you deserve."

Saying this, he shook hands with them both,
and left them with the sedate countenance that
was characteristic of the man.

Edith wrote to her husband, detailing the
watch that appeared to surround Tregarth.
She informed him that the three unmarried
men who formed part of his crew had been
supplied with money, and sent to a distant
port to engage themselves on a foreign voyage;
but that Allen, having a family, had been
detained at home. A report had been spread,
with the view of making his concealment more
secure, that he also had gone on foreign

service, but it was incorrect. She added how much she wished to see him, but on no account to venture into Cornwall until the excitement of the late transactions had subsided. Miss Weston, she told him, was waiting to take that letter, and he might rely on Mr. Weston's assistance. He must not trouble himself about her, because every one was so very kind.

This letter being sealed, and entrusted to Lucy, she accompanied her friend to the quay. She saw her embark, and watched the departing boat until distance and dusky light concealed it from view. She returned home with a more tranquil mind than she had enjoyed for many weeks. Richard was yet safe, and she knew his hiding-place. Time might allay the fierce persecution of the Government, and all might yet be well.

When Lucy arrived at Penwith it was very dark. Her father had been walking on the quay a long time expecting her return, and had become anxious for her safety.

She detailed all the occurrences that transpired at Tregarth, and gave him the letter to be forwarded to Lascare, which was enclosed the day after to Mr. Cleave, with the following epistle from Mr. Weston :—

" Samuel Cleave,

" RESPECTED FRIEND,—I return thee many thanks for thy kindness in sending me the letter addressed to Edith Lascare. I think it requisite thou shouldst be informed that the sailor who solicited that favour of thee is in trouble in consequence of a smuggling transaction, and is unable, at present, to appear in his own locality. His correspondence is in no way connected with that traffic, and relates only to his own safety and domestic affairs. I think it immaterial, both to thee and myself, whether the Government defraud the smuggler, or the smuggler the Government. They both do the same thing in turn. It is dog rob dog. But I am convinced that when the man hath escaped this entanglement he will resort to a sober occupation.

" In the mean time, I think it behoves us to assist his distracted wife, and I shall feel obliged to thee if thou wouldst take the trouble to forward any other communications that may be required.

" I remain,

" Thy sincere friend,

" JONATHAN WESTON."

When Mr. Weston and his daughter talked over these affairs, the very serious aspect of the case became apparent. Whoever fired the fatal shot, the whole crew were aiders and abettors; and unless the Government could be induced to relax the pursuit — although there might be a temporary avoidance of capture—there seemed to be only one inevitable result.

"Could not you, father," said Lucy "apply to those Members of Parliament who represent this place, and ask them, out of common charity, to obtain some mitigation of the punishment, for it could not be said that the deed proceeded from malice?"

"I am afraid, my child, that thou art acquainted with the constitution of thy country in theory only, and art totally ignorant of the reality. The two Members no more represent this town than they represent Pekin. The patron of the borough chooses the Members, or sells to them their seats in Parliament. It is true that they are elected by nine persons, who are called the corporation, but at the dictation of the patron.

"For various reasons—either for past favours or prospective—the Corporation are the slaves of the patron, chosen, as vacancies occur, by the remaining part, as convenient persons to do his service; and not one of them would be so bold or so silly as to ask a favour of the member for their borough. Besides, my dear, at the present moment these two seats are sold, and the patron himself can derive no further profit from the influence of these men."

"Surely," said Lucy, "the people of England do not know this. They cannot know that these Members do not even represent the small constituencies who are said to elect them?"

"I believe not. The people only know a part of the iniquity. They only know that Birmingham and Manchester, and Leeds, and many other large towns, which count their populations by hundreds of thousands, have no representation; and that Penwith—whose name would not be known, but for its bad political eminence — sends two Members to Parliament! The world does not know that the inhabitants have never seen the Members they are supposed to have elected; and he would be a bold man that dared to say publicly that their seats were purchased."

"Why would he be bold?"

"Because he could never prove it. The real actors in this pretty comedy are the agents, and in all probability the principals have never seen each other."

"Perhaps, after all," said Lucy, "the men may be as good as any the patron might choose. It is the system that is bad."

"It is true, my love, that good may sometimes come from evil; and chance might send a good member to Parliament for this ancient borough; but, as a rule, men do not 'gather figs from thorns.' In our present Members we are most unfortunate, for both are interested in the sugar plantations of the West Indies; and one of them, Thomas Potter Macguire, has a multitude of slaves in the island of Jamaica. Penwith is riveting the chains of the poor African slave."

"Is there no such thing, then, as the Commons of England?"

"In reality there is no such thing. The King and the rich landed proprietors govern the country. The popular will, thrown into the scale, will sometimes turn out the governing party, and alter the course of events, but it has no legitimate power."

"Is there any truth," said Lucy, "in the

statement that the system *works* well ? I
see that Castlereagh, in his reply to Francis
Burdett, says that although the representation
of small towns, such as Old Sarum and Gram-
pound, is anomalous, yet he deprecates a meddlesome interference with the Constitution of
this great country, and with a machinery that
may have some isolated imperfections, but is
so excellent in its results."

"I know, my dear, that is what Castlereagh
says, but I believe thou hast put it more
forcibly than the capacity of that weak man
would allow. In simple language it is this,
'don't tamper with machinery that works so
well.' So the drone would say, waiting for
the honey gathered by the industrious bee;
or the reptile watching the store of the
laborious ant. It is for Castlereagh and his
class that it works so well; not for the over-
worked and underfed people. Now, look at
those excellent and happy results. They have
just passed a law that will keep up the war
prices of their estates, and increase the price of
bread to the poor ! They have abolished the
property-tax, which affects themselves, and the
salt-tax, which affects the needy, is allowed
to remain ! "

" But surely," said Lucy, " the rich must pay the salt-tax as well as the poor ? "

" Yes, but not in the same proportion. It is not one per cent. of the rich man's expenditure, of the labourer's wages it is ten. The poor man's diet is salted pork, the rich man's table seldom admits of such homely fare. The natural value of a hundredweight of salt is half-a-crown, the tax raises the price to thirty shillings. In my own business I daily meet with the most oppressive inequalities; and in every instance the weaker the man, the heavier his burden. Some of the more needy persons that transact business with me, draw bills of exchange for no larger amount than five pounds; others, in more thriving circumstances, draw for a hundred. The needy trader pays one shilling for his stamp, the more wealthy three shillings and sixpence; but by the time that the poor man has drawn to the amount of his rich neighbour—as there are twenty fives in a hundred—it has cost him twenty shillings ! In larger amounts the disproportion is still greater. It would take a week to tell you of all their peculations; and yet these people, whose moral turpitude is so great, hang a man for stealing a sheep ! These are the excellent results produced by the machinery that Castle-reagh extols!"

"Then you think," said Lucy, "that nothing can be done for Lascare by any Parliamentary influence?"

"Nothing, my love, by the Members of this place. Any reliance on them would be fatal. Better not to confide in anything than to trust to a broken reed. I would ask William Lemon, the member for our county, to intercede, but he has the rare merit of having been forty years in Parliament, and of never having given a vote for the Government. He is too good a man to have any influence with so bad a set."

CHAPTER XII.

LASCARE conceived that the authorities would keep a watch for him in the sea-ports of the south coast, and that he would be in less danger at Bristol; but even there he was too apprehensive for the enjoyment of security. Instead of isolating himself, he took up his quarters at an inn that was the usual resort of masters of vessels, and assumed the character that belonged to him.

He entered into conversation with the visitors on nautical affairs, which were always uppermost in those establishments, for which, from his long experience and varied information, he was well adapted; and in this manner he passed the first week of his sojourn at Bristol.

He then hoped, by calling on Mr. Cleave, he might receive a reply to his letter, and he accordingly made his way to that gentleman's counting-house.

He was received with great deference by

the person in drab, who occupied the entrance office, whose manners were improved since the first visit, and he was immediately admitted to the private room of the benevolent Quaker.

A smile of satisfaction passed over the countenance of Mr. Cleave as Lascare entered the office. He rose to receive him, and shook hands in a very cordial manner.

"I am glad to see thee, friend, though I neither know thy name, nor wish to know it. If thou art a wise man thou wilt keep both thy name and thy counsel to thyself. Here is a letter, without address, which I have received from Jonathan Weston. I see thou art anxious to know the contents. Though a strong man, thy hand trembles. There, read it, friend, and satisfy thy curiosity. We can talk afterwards."

Lascare took the letter, and his fingers trembled as he broke the seal. It was Edith's own hand-writing. What a pleasure to see it again! He read it through hastily, and gathered the contents of it in general. Afterwards he read it carefully, weighing every word. On the whole it was satisfactory. Then he refolded the letter, so lately written by

Edith. What a gratification at this time was such a letter!

While Lascare was reading, the merchant was replying to his various correspondents; and when he found that the stranger was waiting to speak, he looked up in a listening attitude.

"It is a great relief, sir," said Lascare, "to receive this; and I have to thank you for your great kindness to an utter stranger. I am requested by my friends to remain in this city for a short time, and if you will kindly allow me, I shall trouble you again, and perhaps more than once. I shall never be able to repay you, except with empty thanks; but if it is a gratification to assist an unhappy man, who can neither see his friends nor write to them without danger, you have earned it now."

We frequently read speeches that we should pass by as of an ordinary and commonplace character, but for the effect they have had on the audience. Mr. Cleave, like Quakers in general, professed to be influenced by reason, rather than feeling; but he was much moved by the eloquence of Lascare. It was very ordinary in its style, but it was earnest—there was heart in it—and it touched the feelings of a benevolent man.

"Friend," said the Quaker, "I will not disguise from thee, that if I have been the means of giving thee assistance, my gratification is great; and I tell thee further, that thou mayst use my services as often as thou requirest them. My friend, Jonathan Weston, is interested in thy case, and I hope thou wilt escape from thy difficulties."

Lascare then took leave of the merchant, and retired to reperuse the letter, and reconsider his position.

Other letters passed between him and his wife, of much the same character, and week after week went by in unvarying monotony.

Without occupation, suspecting a spy in every person that particularly noticed him, and reflecting with regret on the fatal shot that had placed him in so hazardous a position, he wandered about the streets and quays of the ancient city in a state of utter dejection. He was alone amidst a multitude, unoccupied in a busy throng, without the social intercourse of an acquaintance or the sympathy of a friend!

His place of residence was also become

uncomfortable. The frequenters of the inn
were too free-and-easy to suit his circumstances. They were communicative on their
own affairs and inquisitive as to the business of
other people.

He remained with them, because a secluded
life might draw attention upon him; but their
boisterous hilarity jarred unpleasantly with
his gloomy feelings, and their prying curiosity
it was difficult to repel.

The length of time he had been hanging
about the inn had begun to create suspicion;
and Lascare observed that when he entered
the room there was frequently a scrutinizing
stare, which the breeding of those sons of
Neptune did not encourage them to disguise.

He would have changed his quarters, but
that involved his leaving the city, for a residence at another house of the same description
would excite additional surprise. If he left
Bristol, he would lose the advantage of the
correspondence with his wife, as he could
hardly expect to find another gentleman so
interested in his behalf as Mr. Cleave.

Nor was his uneasiness without foundation.
The rough manners and noisy conversation of
these men, who gave free utterance to their

thoughts, did not promote the concealment he desired to preserve.

On one occasion during his absence a conversation arose on the idleness of the " dark cap'en," as they called him; and there were various opinions on the mystery that a man of his age should be without occupation, and should be sauntering about the neighbourhood, week after week, for no apparent purpose.

" It's my opinion," said one, " that he's a furriner, though he can spaik English very well; and he may be a Russian spy; but I don't like a man that stares so much at every feller that comes in. It may be that he is looking for some one that he is waiting for, or afraid of somebody that is looking for him. Howsomever, there isn't a drop of English blood in his veins. I saw a black-eyed feller like this at Naples when I was there last. He 'd got nothing to do, and didn't seem to want to do anything; and he was as like this man as two cherries. But give me a man that 'll tell who he is and what he is, and never be ashamed to show his colours."

" I believe," said another, " that the feller's bin up to something bad. I saw a vessel sail out of Genoa last year with another such cap'en as that—a dark, curly-headed fellow; and there wasn't a man in the port that didn't believe he was algerening. She was a long, rakish craft, with narrow beams and tall spars. A vessel that's built without stowage enough for a lighter and spars enough for a frigate is up to no good."

"Ah! many a poor feller," said a third, "has been nabbed between Genoa and the Straits. They sail, but we never hear of 'em after. Likely enough they found their last port at Algiers. 'Tis time the Government should look after that d—d place."

Lascare heard nothing of this, or he might have thought it was time to quit the society of such uncongenial companions. His disposition was not intrusive, and his circumstances imposed a cautious reserve; still he entered into conversation with them on nautical affairs, and gave his opinion and related his experience with great freedom. His seamanship was not doubted, but the nature of the craft he had commanded was a matter of suspicion, and his dark fiery eye, and swarthy complexion were indications of a paternity beyond the British isles.

A few days after this conversation the noisy

sailors were again taking their evening glass, and Lascare was present. One after the other they spoke of the proceedings of the day. Some told of the quantity of their cargoes unshipped or loaded, others of cargoes on offer, the amount of the freight, the demurrage expected, and all the various topics connected with their pursuit.

"I've come 'ere with a cargo of Valonia from the Mediterranean, and I've bin lyin' 'ere a fortnight, but I havn't seen your ship, Cap'en."

This was said to Lascare as four others were sitting at the table, drinking their ale and smoking their pipes. There had been some previous conversation among them touching the whereabouts of Lascare's craft, and this sudden observation aroused general attention.

"I have the misfortune," said Lascare, "to be out of a berth for the present, and I'm waiting here to see if anything will turn up."

At this the previous speaker took the long pipe from his mouth, and expelled a continuous stream of smoke, closing one eye, and smiling contemptuously.

The reply, and the incredulity evinced by the inquiring captain, raised a burst of merriment among the others, in which Lascare felt it policy to join, remarking that "they were on the laughing side now, but he hoped it wouldn't be long."

"It won't be long for me," said another, "for I'm off to-morrow for Cardiff. My ship's the Eliza, and come 'ere from Odessa, with a cargo of corn."

"Rough passage that Black Sea passage," chimed in a third (eager to show his experience, and greatly to the relief of Lascare, who wished the topic to be changed). "The last time that I was out there we had a gale that struck the ship on her beam ends, and I thought we should never see land again. However, she righted after a while ; but they won't catch me out there again if I can help it."

There was one who had not spoken, but seemed by his attention to encourage his companions. He was a swarthy, thin-featured man, that had a lowering, cut-throat expression, more dangerous, the smuggler thought, than the coarse bluster of the rest.

"A fellow, by the hand of Nature marked,
Quoted, and signed, to do a deed of shame."

As evening wore on Lascare detected his

furtive glances directed towards himself, and they brought to his recollection the reward of a hundred pounds offered to any one who would give information leading to the apprehension of any of the crew of the Swift. Edith had drawn his attention to this advertisement in her last letter, and cautioned him to be on his guard.

Lascare retired to his room, but it was morning before he could sleep, and he came down to breakfast but little refreshed by his night's rest. The sour, repulsive visage of the swarthy captain haunted him in his dreams.

In the morning he did not see the thin, spare man, with the gloomy aspect, and his apprehension subsided. He conceived that his critical position, and the fears that naturally attended it, had magnified an ill-favoured countenance into the diabolical, and smiled now at the spectre his imagination had conjured up.

In the forenoon he went to the office of Mr. Cleave for a letter that he expected. It was waiting for him, and brought the joyful information that, at a meeting of the leading smugglers, it was thought that he might return to his home, but the greatest caution was recommended.

This opinion was founded on the discontinuance of the efforts made for his apprehension, and an abatement of the sensation the late event had produced; but he was advised to take the north Devon and north Cornwall route, and to enter Tregarth, after dark, by the western road.

"I shall trouble you once more," he said to Mr. Cleave. "I am recommended to go home, and to-morrow I will bring my last letter, announcing my departure, and take my leave."

"I am pleased," said the merchant, "that thy affairs have taken a favourable turn; and, under the circumstances, I shall be glad to say farewell to thee."

Lascare left the office with the intention of returning the next day, and of thanking the kind-hearted gentleman for the warm interest he had taken on his behalf. But he never did it! Mr. Cleave never again saw Richard Lascare!

A week after her letter had been despatched Edith daily expected an answer, detailing the course he intended to pursue; but she waited in vain! She became anxious, sometimes thinking he would arrive without notice, and sometimes thinking some evil had befallen him.

Night after night she listened, and as a foot-step on the highway approached the door she laid down her work and watched the latch, but the walker went on.

Anxiety, expectation, and disappointment waited on her daily. She would not leave the house, fearing Richard might arrive in her absence; but day after day went on, and week succeeded week, without any intelligence of Lascare.

John and Mary Spillar sat with her till late every night, and that continued so long that it was at length agreed that Mr. Weston should be requested to inquire of his Bristol friend when the missing sailor was last seen.

Edith wrote to Lucy, giving her a full account of her expectations and disappoint-ments, and requesting that Mr. Weston would communicate with Mr. Cleave.

This was immediately attended to, and within a week a reply was received from that gentleman, giving a circumstantial account of their last interview. He was as much surprised and bewildered as the people of Tregarth. Lascare had never named his place of residence to him, nor was it a case in which inquiry could be safely made, because it might prove fatal to his concealment.

He related also that two persons had afterwards called, inquiring for a man that answered his description, and that the pursuit of these might be connected with his mysterious disappearance; but he believed the immediate object of these men had been baffled.

The merchant's reply was most unsatisfactory. A month passed away, and Edith feared some accident had befallen him. All kinds of terrific visions were floating in her mind. Sometimes he was fleeing for refuge from his native land, sometimes he was gasping the name of Edith in his last throes, and she was not there.

All Lascare's friends who had been entrusted with the secret were in a state of despondency. At first it was whispered outside of the trusted circle that the smuggler had disappeared in a mysterious manner. Rumour made the calamity more certain, and it was asserted, with great assurance, that he had been accidentally drowned.

This latter report had taken so tenacious a hold of the public mind, and the general regret was so openly avowed, that when it reached the family of Mr. Weston, they thought Edith had received information of the event by another route.

"Thou shalt go, my dear, to Tregarth," said Mr. Weston, "and offer the poor child a home. Full of calamity as the world is, misery like this seldom comes to one in the flower of life, and still less frequently to one bereft—or who seems to be bereft—of every relative on earth."

Lucy's eyes were filled with tears on hearing this, because her father seemed convinced of the truth of the report, and because she feared the effect of such a catastrophe on the mind of her susceptible friend.

"I thank you, my dear father," said she, "for the suggestion, and I will see Edith to-morrow; but I hope it is not true."

"So do I, my love; but they are giving such circumstantial accounts of the place where it happened, that there is more truth to be apprehended than one could wish."

At this moment the door opened, and Rachel entered the room, looking very important, as if she had some weighty information to impart.

"Hast thee heard that the smuggler that married Edith Phinn hath drowned hisself?"

"No, Rachel. The account I heard was that he was drowned by accident."

"Then the news is come now that he drowned hisself. I was sure something bad would come to that man. He never married Edith Phinn with *my* consent. A harum-scarum fellow that tried to drown hisself once is sure to do it again."

"I don't think, Rachel," said Mr. Weston, "that Lascare ever tried to drown himself."

"'Tis the same thing, if he went to say when it was a tempting o' Providence to go. Poor thing! She loved the man. I don't grieve for Dick Lascare, but for that poor lamb that is left alone in the world."

"I am going to see her to-morrow, and will bring her here if the news is true," said Lucy.

"I thought thee wouldst, my dear. I love her, next to thee, as my own child."

Here good old Rachel's sobbing prevented further utterance; and Lucy, who had somewhat recovered, again wept in company. Even old Mr. Weston felt the contagion, and, to prevent an exhibition of weakness, left the room without remark.

CHAPTER XIII.

WHEN Lascare left the office of Mr. Cleave, he looked suddenly along the street through which he had walked on coming to the place, and at the corner saw the ill-favoured captain whose furtive glances of the previous evening had given him a troubled night. It was evident that the spy did not immediately see him; for as Lascare walked down on one side. his look was intently fixed on the other.

At length the person of Lascare was recognized, and immediately the other hastily made off; and, by the time the smuggler had reached the corner, his acquaintance was nowhere to be seen.

Before this new encounter with the suspected person, Lascare had reasoned himself into the belief that his apprehensions were due more to his perilous position than to any evil designs of the dark-visaged captain, but now he felt assured that his movements had been watched, and that at any moment his person might be seized.

He instantly determined to forsake the suspected residence, leaving his kit to balance the landlord's account; and if there should be a watch for his return, they would be disappointed of their prize.

He walked with great rapidity in a direction opposite to his usual course, harassed with the painful feeling that an enemy dogged his heels.

Just at this moment a hackney-coach was passing, which the smuggler hailed; and the driver was directed to proceed, with great despatch, to a quarter of the city remote from his former residence, but well known to Lascare.

He watched from the carriage-window all the vehicles that were behind, but could discover nothing that had the appearance of pursuit.

The man waiting at the corner of the street had seen Lascare enter the premises of Mr. Cleave, but, from some inattention, did not notice his exit; and he was walking at a good pace down on the opposite side before his eye caught him. When he saw the object of his watch he turned the corner, and concealed himself in one of those numerous waggon-yards that were then so common, but which the

goods-stations of the railways have now super-
seded, with the view of following him to any
other of his haunts. The object of this
espionage was, if possible, to satisfy his mind
that his suspicion was well founded before he
pounced upon his prey.

He waited a considerable time, but the man
did not pass; and when he emerged from his
hiding-place, and looked along the street,
Lascare was not in view.

Blaming himself for not taking more active
measures, and fearing that the quarry might
escape, he proceeded at once to lay an information before the clerk of the magistrates;
and produced a hand-bill offering a hundred
pounds reward for the apprehension of any
of the crew of the Swift, and detailing the
personal appearance of each. This he had
procured at Tinmouth, on the south of Devon,
and had brought it with him into the north
channel, with a soul craving for the gold.

Lascare was a marked character, such as
was not likely to be mistaken; and the official
being satisfied of the probability of his capture,
a warrant was issued for his apprehension.

The informer and the detective—they were
not policemen in those days—proceeded to the

Fountain Inn, and waited for the smuggler, who habitually arrived there at noon. The man did not appear. They waited till three o'clock, and were disappointed. The constable then recommended a visit to the house the fugitive had been seen to enter.

When they arrived the inquisitive doorkeeper inquired their business. Thinking, in so respectable an establishment, to have all the aid possible in the furtherance of justice, they related to the demure, and apparently obtuse, Quaker the object of their call. Never did they meet with a man of so forgetful a memory, or who was so confused with a description. He inquired and listened. So many people had called, that he could scarcely remember individuals. Had they tried any other place? Had they waited at his lodgings? All his inquiries being answered, he left them in the anteroom while he communicated with his master.

Mr. Cleave felt regret that an escape which seemed so near had not been accomplished, but it relieved his mind that, as Lascare had not returned to his quarters at the usual time, there was a probability that he knew of their pursuit. He therefore thought that the detention of his foes was the best means of aiding him, and he endeavoured to protract their visit as long as prudence would permit.

He sent out a message requesting that they would seat themselves until he had concluded some important correspondence, when he should be glad to communicate with them.

When he conceived that a further delay might excite suspicion he rang the bell, and ordered his servant to show them in.

When they entered he desired them to be seated, and then inquired the object of their visit.

The municipal officer then explained that they were in the pursuit of a murderer, and had information that he had visited Mr. Cleave's establishment on the morning of that day. The hand-bill giving a description of the person of Lascare, and offering the reward of a hundred pounds for the apprehension of either of the crew, was shown, and the Quaker perused the document, deliberately and attentively.

The height, person, and visage of the smuggler were so minutely described, that Mr. Cleave did not hesitate to believe, with the additional evidence of Lascare's own statement, that they were in pursuit of the right man.

He now turned to the informer and engaged him in conversation, which was frequently interrupted by the constable, in the hope of terminating the interview; but the Quaker persistently returned to the subject with further interrogations; and his dupe, proud of being the repository of so much information, was very voluble and lengthy in his replies.

"From thy account I gather," said Mr. Cleave, "that the smuggler shot a man, who was about to take his property or to shoot him. One wicked deed was committed to prevent another; but there appears to have been no malice aforethought. Very praiseworthy, perhaps, of thee to take so much trouble in the cause of justice."

The sailor made no remark.

"Oh! I see," said the other, pretending to take another look at the handbill; "thou wilt have a reward. Not thirty pieces of silver— that was once the price of blood, but one hundred pieces of gold. The difference, friend, is in the number of pieces, and the metal; it is all the same—the price of blood! Judas went out *afterwards* and hanged himself. I don't advise, thee, friend, to hang thyself, but, if thou art going to do such a thing, I think it would be a benefit to society if thou wouldst hang thyself *first*."

The sailor trembled that the avarice of his soul was laid bare, and made no reply.

At this point the constable began to be aware that valuable time was passing, and that Mr. Cleave had not yet given any information, but had wormed out all that they themselves could give. He thought that there should be a little reciprocity, and he asked that gentleman, rather brusquely, if the man who had been with him had curly hair.

"Yes, he had," said Mr. Cleave ; "but I don't know that thou couldst derive any certainty from that, for I could show thee three or four of my clerks whose locks curl marvellously, either by a freak of Nature, or by a process of hot irons."

"May I ask, sir, what his business was with you ? "

"Thou mayst ask, friend ; but we mercantile men do not think it prudent to communicate to others the nature of any business we may transact."

"Do you mean to say that you will not tell the nature of the business before a court of justice ?"

" Thou mayst perceive, I think, that we are not in a court of justice; and when we get there, then we shall see. I don't think, either, that thy commission entitles thee to act in the capacity of a judge."

"You must excuse me, Mr. Cleave—for plainness is better than politeness—that I think your conduct is very much like aiding and abetting a murderer."

" I don't know that I am bound to excuse an impertinent remark. Whilst agreeing with thee that plainness is better than politeness, I like them *best* united."

They had now arrived at a point at which further conversation was undesirable for either party; and Mr. Cleave, seeing, with gratification, the shades of evening approaching, bade his two friends farewell.

With night at hand, and thinking it useless at that time to make any further out-door search, they returned to the Fountain, with the determination, if the object of their pursuit should not be there, to wait his arrival.

They inquired of the landlord if the carpet-bag of the dark captain remained in his room; and being informed that it was still there, they settled themselves in the coffee-room, expecting every moment the appearance of Lascare.

When the carriage that conveyed the fugitive had arrived at the place appointed the coachman's fare was paid, and Lascare had the satisfaction to observe that he took a different direction towards his home.

His next purpose was to disguise his person, which he did very effectually, so far as external effect was concerned; for an outfitter supplied him with a rough monkey-jacket and a sou'-wester, which gave him the appearance of one whose berth was before the mast, rather than in the vicinity of the state cabin.

He also cut off those black, curly locks that hung almost to his shoulders, and he was so altered that an intimate acquaintance might not have known him.

Thus metamorphosed he sought a neighbourhood suitable to his new character, and arrived at a low public-house on the quay. His object was to leave Bristol as soon as possible, and not to be fastidious as to his destination.

He discovered there was a vessel that had cleared for sailing on that night bound for Newport. One of the crew was sipping his ale and smoking his pipe; and Lascare, who had before mixed generally with the sailors, sat down beside him.

"Well, comrade," said the strange sailor, "where d' ye hail from?"

"From Golant, in the west."

"What are ye driving at?"

"Looking out for a passage to Wales, where I can ship aboard a collier bound for a Devonshire port."

"Our skipper can give ye a berth if he likes."

"If he will," said Lascare, "I will work my passage and carry my grub."

"Then come with me, and I'll spaik to the cap'en."

The two sailors left the place of entertainment together, smoking their short pipes, with the indifference of men who were satisfied with the past and careless for the future; and they came alongside the Bessie, of Chester, then bound for Newport, and waiting only for the turn of the tide. The captain allowed Lascare to take his passage, and the vessel of refuge floated down the stream, lessening the weight of the fugitive's mind as the distance from the ancient city increased.

While the flowing sail of the Bessie was conveying the good ship to Wales, the sailor's absence from his old quarters was a matter of disappointment and surprise.

Waiting for him in the coffee-room of the Fountain, while he floated down the Severn, was the scowling captain, whose malice was depicted in his fiendish countenance, and sitting beside him was the Bristol detective.

They appeared to be men having no unusual business in hand, and they sipped their ale while they joined in conversation on the different topics of the day. When the usual time of Lascare's appearance had passed, and there was no sign of his approach, they looked significantly at each other, but said nothing. They waited on and on. Dark night was come, but not the missing captain. Anxious to secure the promised reward, the informer detained the constable till ten o'clock, when the latter determined to wait no longer.

"I'm afraid," said the spy, "the devil saw me in Southport Street."

"Nothing more likely," replied the disappointed detective, who, with lowering eyebrows, smiled contemptuously.

"What do you main?" said the sailor.

" That if you was in Southport Street the
devil was there, and in every other street you
went through. He's a gentleman that dances
close attendance upon such as you, and nabs
them at last. He must have owed me a grudge,
to keep me here to this time of night. Now,
I 'll tell 'ee what. 'Tis my business to look
after this sort of craft, and I git my lawful
livin' by it ; but when a fella tries to trap his
own messmate or a brother chip, the devil's
too good company for en. You 've got malice
enough, but haven't brains enough for your
dirty work."

" You don't main to say that you 'll give
up the chase ? " said the informer.

" No ; but your precious bungling has made
it almost a hopeless one. If he hadn't known
that we 'm in pursuit, he would have been
here. Starting from this place, he 's got all
the points of the compass to choose. I can
follow but one. He may be off to the north-
east, while I am going south-west to seek
him ! "

Saying this, the enraged constable, excited
by drink and vexation, left the greedy informer
in disappointment and dismay.

The next morning inquiry was made at all

the booking-offices if a sailor answering to the description, had taken his place by any stage-coach, but without obtaining any satisfactory clue. Some wondering grooms thought they had seen him; but in a more minute description, the likeness failed in some important point.

Relinquishing the land routes, as offering insufficient grounds for pursuit, the constable started for the quays, and visited all the haunts of the "sailor on shore." Here he was equally disappointed: for whether he was lying perdu, or had taken his departure, it was equally impossible to determine. More than a dozen vessels had left by the evening tide, bound to as many ports, and no knowledge of their crews could be ascertained. The prying official returned in disgust, to relate to his chief the failure of the pursuit.

CHAPTER XIV.

The Bessie had a favourable passage to Newport, in Monmouthshire, and nothing transpired to indicate that Lascare was not what he
appeared. He parted from his new acquaintances when they arrived in port, and, instead
of taking up his abode at a public-house, he
succeeded in obtaining lodgings suitable to
the character he had assumed. He pretended
that his occupation was on the quays, where
he passed a great part of his time; being careful
to take his meals at workmanlike hours. He
was not now subject to any disagreeable inquiries, and the landlady, having regular pay
and little trouble, was satisfied with her guest.

There he remained some weeks, without
taking any active measures for his security;
fearing to take the journey that had been recommended, on account of the suspicion that had
been excited at Bristol, and dreading to en-
trust a letter to the post-office until he had
determined to quit his present abode.

At length he conceived that he could prudently let Edith know that he was safe; and, to prevent the possibility of being traced by the post-mark, if the letter should fall into hostile hands, he left Newport on the day it was posted.

The morning after the discussion that related to the death of Lascare, Lucy Weston was preparing for her departure to Tregarth, when her father entered the parlour with a letter in his hand.

"There is more cause for thy voyage, my dear, than I expected. Here is a letter for Edith, brought by post this morning, a message of either good or evil import. The cover is addressed to me, and within there is neither date nor the name of the place from which it was despatched, but the post-mark is Newport."

"It is Lascare's writing," said Lucy, joyfully; "I shall be the most welcome messenger to-day that ever carried glad tidings to a sorrowful heart."

She immediately embarked with two good boatmen, who dashed the little boat through the sea with such vigour, that she quickly landed on Leyland beach, from which she took the footpath by the shore, leaving the boatmen to wait her return.

This precaution was necessary, for the ladies of Tregarth — although good people in the main — were busybodies, and a landing at the quay would be known throughout the place before Lucy could reach Edith's abode, and speculation would be rife relating to the object of her visit. By the land route she would pass through a very small portion of the town, and would escape the scrutinizing gaze and the tattling remarks of the inquisitive bevy. For, besides the inconvenience of such popular attention, it was desirable that the name of Lascare should have as little mention as possible, and that the gossipping sisterhood should have no cause for wondering at the message she might bring.

On arriving at Tregarth, Lucy found her friend in a state of deep dejection, and she feared the consequences of a too sudden re-action. She had a beautiful, but brittle vessel to deal with, which must be handled with the greatest tenderness. Lascare was made the subject of conversation, and Lucy related the stories that were afloat, which Edith knew were without foundation. She imparted the information that he was alive and well, very gradually, and delayed for some time the full confirmation.

At length she produced the proof in his own hand-writing.

The news was told quite fast enough. The sensitive young wife, in her eagerness, could with difficulty open the letter, or read its contents.

" Allow me to open and read it for you," said Lucy, taking the letter into her own hand. She scanned the letter, giving information as she cast her eyes hastily over it.

" Richard is well, you will see him in a short time, perhaps within a week. There, that is the substance. Now you can read it for yourself."

It was dated from Newport, in Wales, stated that he was well, that he should leave that town immediately, and that he hoped to arrive home by the route she recommended, when he would explain the cause of his detention.

The letter was written on coarse paper, and was very short, and the writing—compared with the clear hand he usually wrote—was a scrawl. It was evidently written at a place where pens and paper were not in frequent requisition.

Edith read and re-read it; wondered where he was then, and what kind of residence he was in when he wrote that letter; where and how he was travelling at that very moment, and when she might expect him. Her reverie was broken by Lucy.

"Now then, as soon as you have given me something to eat I will return. I must not forget that my boatmen are waiting."

"Will you forgive me for not asking you before?" said Edith, surprised at her inattention.

"Yes, upon one condition—that you do exactly what I tell you. In the first place, after I am gone, send for Mr. Spillar. He may not be at home, or may be detained. When that sagacious old man arrives he will set you right; but if, in the mean time, you should disclose that elation that you now feel, you may unintentionally give currency to a report that Richard is safe, and that may endanger his security."

"I will not leave the house, but will send to him," said Edith. "If John Spillar should not be at home, I will wait till he comes."

"That is something," said Lucy, feeling the contagion of Edith's delight, and her old pleasant satire returning; "that is something, certainly, so far as it shows that you will not publish your secret to the whole world. When I came, you were looking like a widow, and with more sorrows than the most of them feel; *now* you are something like a bride, painting in her imagination the prettiest pictures of marriage bliss, that stoics tell us will never be realized. If any should observe the change, won't they think that you have had favourable news ?"

"You are right, my dear Lucy, you are always right; and I will try to do all you recommend, although I could more easily put on a bright countenance when I am sad, than I can look mournful when I am feeling so happy."

Lucy partook of the refreshments that Edith had now busily prepared, and afterwards returned to Penwith, where the Westons enjoyed the news that was unknown to the busy and meddlesome world.

John Spillar arrived at Edith's cottage soon after Lucy's departure. He thought Lascare could not arrive earlier than five days from that time, and it was possible that he might find it necessary to take a still more circuitous route.

While these proceedings were going on in Cornwall, Lascare had taken his first step towards his return.

He embarked on board a coal vessel bound for Biddeford, and the day after his arrival he took the coast road through the north of Devon. Sometimes he had a lift in a stage-van, and then again he would take a long day's walk. In this manner he travelled through Torrington, Stratton, and Bude, and arrived at his last resting-place on the north coast, which was the far-famed castle of Tintagel. Very few travellers at that time went by the northern route, for the sea-side mania was not at its height and the beautiful inlets of that rocky shore were as solitary as they were wild.

Hitherto he had met with nothing that aroused suspicion, but now a more wary and watchful conduct became necessary. He slept through the night at the village of Tintagel, and starting early in the morning, he took his zigzag journey towards the south. He avoided all the larger towns, and leaving the Cheesewring on the right, he passed all the moorland district before dusk, and took what should be called the lanes, rather than the roads, that led towards the coast. Before dark night had set in he arrived at roads that were well known to him, and, unless his foes were watching his home, his arrival would be safe.

When the days were drawing near that Lascare might be expected, John and Mary Spillar paid a visit to Edith's cottage as their last duty before retiring to rest. This they did for the purpose of seeing whether her husband had arrived, and of cheering up her failing hope as night after night passed away in disappointment.

Edith seemed to forget, in the hopeful prospect of meeting her husband, that there was danger still lurking around their home. Without being able to tell on what night he might appear, for two evenings previous to that event she prepared for his coming, in the arrangement of a well-furnished board to greet his arrival, for she wisely conceived that fatigue of body and mental excitement would require all her contrivances to refresh him.

Very prudently, also, those acquainted with the secret refrained from remaining with Edith after night had set in, feeling that the first meeting of the loving pair would be more agreeable unobserved; and good old John Spillar, with Mary, his wife, believing that the time had arrived when Lascare might be expected, left the house early.

Two of those nights had passed by, and Richard had not come; but Edith felt certain on this, the third night, that before morning her husband would embrace her again.

There alone she sat on, trying to knit, the little fire burning blithely the while. The dusk of evening had passed, but he had not come. Then she blamed herself for her impatience.

"Richard cannot come to the neighbourhood," she thought, "till darkness conceals his features. At this moment he may be miles away. Oh! that the time may come when we can live together in peace, that I may enjoy the society of my noble husband without the anxiety that haunts me now. Hark! there are footsteps approaching. 'Tis the return of our weary neighbour, carrying on his back the fuel for the evening fire. Hard lot! Nothing for to-morrow's food but the earnings of to-day. Yet he fears no ambush. He eats his crust in peace. Too low to be envied, too poor to be robbed, he sleeps well."

One hour after the other of watching and waiting, waiting and watching, passed away.

"Surely," she thought, "I heard a sound! Is there some one outside the window? Listen again. All is silent. 'Tis my own fancy, my own disturbed imagination. I will try to be quiet. It is better that I should wait than he should risk being observed. I hear it again! There may be some one about the house."

She opened the door, and stood in the doorway, looking out. There was nothing to be seen.

Standing nearly opposite—but concealed by the brambles and the darkness of the night—was Richard Lascare! He stood motionless, watching her, admiring her. He was not worthy of her, he thought.

In another instant she was in the strong arms of her husband. The stalwart man lifted her light weight within the threshold, closed the door, and embraced his loving wife.

Edith was in his arms before she saw him; but she knew it was Richard. She had been lifted by that powerful arm before, and she was too happy for speech.

Many seconds passed before they spoke, but the tears fell fast. Even the hard, weather-

beaten sailor, full of resolute daring, and unused
—even in cases when feeling was strong—to
yield to womanly tears, wept as he hung over
the tearful countenance of his lovely wife.

Love and joy, fear and apprehension were
mingled together. How long could they enjoy
each others' society? When must they part
again? Is there a spy watching at the
door?

It was a stolen pleasure, sweet while it
lasted. How long was it to last?

"Oh, Richard, Richard! I was afraid we
should never meet again. Will our troubles
never end; or what end will they have?"

Lascare tried to smile away her fears, but it
was a feeble attempt. She saw the effort, but
was not deceived by it. She looked into his
face. It was smitten with care and privation.
The long curling locks were gone. The canvas
trousers and the long rough jacket told their
own tale. The sou'-wester lay on the floor, as
if it had done its work and its service was
ended.

She took the whole in at a glance.

"I see it all, Richard," she said, "and am
grateful. Now take what you can eat and
drink. I must be a man to help you, not a

poor, frail woman. I was born to save, not to be a burden to you."

At this time the footsteps of their aged foster-parents were heard at the door. The latch lifted, and in walked the tall, spare figure of John Spillar, and the stiff and stately Mary, with a countenance beaming with pleasure. She outstripped her husband when she saw how affairs were inside, and kissed her dear boy, as she called him.

Old John repressed the emotion he felt, shook Lascare warmly by the hand, and welcomed him home.

The cause of the sudden discontinuance of the correspondence was now explained, but the revelation rather added to their distrust. They spent the night together till a late hour; and when the old couple left, they urged the necessity that the utmost secrecy should be observed.

CHAPT ERXV.

AFTER the agitation caused by Lascare's return had somewhat subsided, he explained to Edith and his more intimate friends the cause of his detention and change of residence, and the continued silence he thought it necessary to adopt. He also recounted the incidents of his journey home; and, although he discovered that no one was on the watch for him, he was frequently in alarm.

He feared a recognition if he came to his house earlier, and also, whether a foe might not be waiting his arrival.

He listened at the door, and at the window; and unconscious what the silence within might mean, he slunk back, to be shielded from view by the darkness of the hedge, when he heard a person moving towards the door. Long they talked of the past, and long of their hopes and fears.

They discoursed anxiously of their future proceedings; but they determined, above all, that for some time Lascare's return must be a secret.

About a month after his arrival, it became known to the inhabitants of Tregarth that Lascare had returned, and many of his old acquaintances called to see him. There was no fear of the coast-guard, for they dared not arrest him; and the smugglers found means to obtain secret information if any movement should be directed by the authorities. Still both he and Allen, the mate, remained watchful at home, and both relied on the hope that the cessation of the trade would induce the Government to forego their punishment.

After a while they walked openly in the streets, but did not wander far from Tregarth.

Suddenly a meeting of the secret council was convened, and information was laid before them that an active pursuit of Allen and Lascare was in preparation. Means were adopted to procure their concealment, and they resorted to the most certain methods of acquiring the earliest information of the course the Board of Customs intended to pursue.

It should be related, to the honour of the

smugglers, that although lust of gain, and the excitement always attendant on great hazard, had induced them to unite for the employment of others in their precarious occupation, they never failed, in the expenditure of time or money, to protect them when they had arrived at the extremity of their dangerous pursuit.

One fine day, when the busy inhabitants were engaged in their various occupations, and a bevy of women were sitting on the rocks by the sea-side, thriftily knitting the blue worsted hose and the guernsey frock, while the sea dashed its white foam in harmless fury below, a troop of dragoons rode down their steep and dangerous road. Not daring to put their horses to the trot, they slowly guided them over a declivity that would endanger the step of a Spanish mule.

Instantly the astonished and terrified women rose from their labours! Never before had such a spectacle as this appeared at Tregarth! The horses, the helmets, the flowing crests, and the dangling swords, were objects of astonishment and dread.

The frightened steeds were prancing in a street in which it was difficult to stand and dangerous to move. The alarmed inmates of the houses crowded to the doors and windows, while a multitude of terrified urchins ran on before and surprised all beyond.

When the soldiers arrived at the middle of the town, a detachment took a different course, and rode directly to the house of Edward Allen, while the main body continued in a straight direction—if any of their meandering streets can be called straight—to the residence of Lascare.

Now the crowd, suspecting the object of their visit, followed close behind, and watched with anxiety the result.

When the troop arrived at the smuggler's dwelling, the officer in command alighted and tapped gently at the door. It was speedily opened, and a venerable man stood at the entrance, with mild, but undaunted countenance. A feeling of disappointment pervaded the features of the soldier as he looked at the hoary locks and undismayed bearing of the handsome old man.

It was evident to him this was not the object of his search.

"I have called," said he, "to know if Richard Lascare is within?"

" He is not, sir," replied the veteran sailor; " home and Richard Lascare have been very little acquainted of late."

" May I ask your name ? "

" My name is John Spillar."

" It is my duty to search this house. Numbers one and two, dismount, and make the search."

I hope," said Spillar, " your commission will enable you to treat the sailor's wife with respect ? "

" You may rely on it," said the officer, " that they will not exceed their duty."

Edith remained sitting at the table, listening with composed countenance to the conversation, as the soldiers entered.

" This," said Spillar, " is Richard Lascare's wife. I hope that her name is not included in the warrant."

The young officer was struck with the remarkable beauty of her countenance—never more lovely than as she sat, with mild and resigned features, while the soldiers ransacked the premises. He advanced, and bowing respectfully, said, " I am sorry that the disagreeable duty has devolved upon me of entering your house so rudely; but you may rely on it that no more disturbance shall be made than is absolutely necessary."

"Thank you," said Edith, mildly. "I am sorry that it has been thought necessary to send you here; but if you seek my husband, he is not at home."

That this reply was genuine the commander did not doubt. It was spoken with a composure that was entirely free from apprehension, which it was impossible in such circumstances to assume, and the return of the disappointed soldiers verified the statement.

The demeanour of Edith awed the officer into feelings of respect; surprised to find a gentlewoman in such a place and under such circumstances; and, again apologizing for his apparent rudeness, and bowing politely, he ordered the two dragoons to remount.

The same kind of success had met the other soldiers at Allen's; and the whole company departed from the little town by the road they had entered, accompanied by a multitude of men, women, and children, who followed them up the ascent until they arrived at a less dangerous road, when, spurring their horses, they soon disappeared among the hills and vallies of that mountainous coast.

This was the first attempt to seize the smugglers at Tregarth; and, as it was known that they walked openly in the streets, there was no fear entertained on the part of the authorities of the result.

The Board of Customs had determined to arrest the sailors who formed part of the crew of the Swift that remained at home; and, knowing that the Coast-guard were unable to make the seizure, they applied to the commander-in-chief for assistance.

The military governor of the nearest garrison was directed to supply any troops that might be required, and this force was despatched, being previously supplied with the information necessary, and a plan of the town, in which the houses of Lascare and Allen were particularly marked, with a warrant to arrest those two men, and convey them to a place of security.

It was known that they resided at their own houses at Tregarth, and might on any occasion be taken into custody. But the smugglers had learnt a lesson from their past experience. They had discovered that information was the great lever of success, and that the officials had no aversion to the gold that had been acquired by the contraband trade.

No sooner was it resolved to send the military, than the brotherhood at Tregarth became acquainted with the determination. The men were therefore dismissed to safe places of concealment, and two of the leaders were selected to be present with their wives at the time the military might be expected to arrive.

The commander of the troop, having understood that there was a certainty of their apprehension, conceived that his duty was to seize and guard the offenders; but he returned to his quarters in disappointment and disgust. It was clear that their intended visit had been previously known and carefully provided for; and that the information must have emanated from some Government department.

The secret of the expected visit was well kept by the smugglers. The inhabitants at first were surprised and dismayed; but they were considerably relieved at seeing the dragoons depart, surly with disappointment.

The authorities were greatly displeased on reading the report of the commanding officer, relating that the secret of their intended journey had been divulged; that the men had been secretly conveyed to a place unknown;

and that respectable persons waited at their respective houses to watch the proceedings.

The two smugglers had received many hours' notice of the intended capture, and proceeded to their hiding-places previously provided; and the morning after they returned to their homes, and remained for some months unmolested.

But the Board of Customs had by no means relinquished the determination to secure these noted men, and they left them for a time in fancied security, that they might the more easily entrap them at last.

It was some months after the attempt recorded that the two men were strolling together on the hill, when information was brought of the approach of a party of dragoons, and in the hurry of their departure they started without any previous arrangement.

They left Tregarth by the western road, about half-an-hour before the military made its appearance.

The commander was made acquainted by a spy, who watched the fugitives, with the course they had taken. He put his troop to the gallop, until the steepness of the road com-

pelled them to bring their panting horses to a
walk.

About a mile from Tregarth a road running
north and south crossed their way. At this
part, called the Four Lane End, they divided
into three parties, and again increased their
speed. One party continued its onward course,
while the two others diverged to the roads
lying in opposite directions.

It happened that at this crossing the two
smugglers had agreed to take different routes,
the one leading into the country, and the other
towards the coast.

The cavalry made great speed on the land
side; but while the soldiers urged their horses
along the road, Allen lay concealed in a furze-
brake, listening to their conversation, and
hearing the grateful sound of their horses' hoofs
as they scampered at a distance from their
prey.

Concealment was not his only resource, for
if he had been brushed from cover, he would
have bounded down a rugged steep, where it
was impossible for cavalry to follow, and that
terminated in a deep ravine covered by brushwood, under which he could have proceeded
either way unobserved. There was no necessity

for bringing that resource under requisition. He lay perfectly still, and in less than an hour had the satisfaction to hear the troop returning at a slow pace, grumbling with vexation over their disappointment.

No appearance of security tempted him to move out until night had set in, and then it was with cautious steps and at a late hour that he crept towards his home.

The road which Lascare took led, in the first place, to a farm-yard; but there were fields between that and the coast through which he must pass, with the view of concealing himself in the thick brushwood that fringed the shore. Here there would have been a safe retreat, if time had allowed him to choose the most suitable place; but, unfortunately, he heard the horses approaching before he could perfectly conceal himself, and by the time he had crept beneath the thicket, the soldiers had entered on the open field above.

He was too near the margin of the cover to be safe; for there was no doubt that they would explore all the higher portion, if they did not venture into the brambles below. Still he crept downward, and as they came nearer he lay perfectly still.

They dismounted, and leaving some to guard the horses, they proceeded along the edge of the thicket, and as they went on, they turned their backs to the place where Lascare had made his entrance, peering into every rabbit-creep for the smuggler's trail. As they increased their distance, Lascare crept nearer to the shore, and at length arrived at the verge of the cliff. Here was a steep and dangerous descent to the beach and the rocks below. In order to lessen his speed in sliding down this precipice, he held on by a twig, but its rebound, when he relinquished his hold, was seen by the soldiers above, who shouted like a pack of hounds in full cry. They had not seen Lascare, but they knew that some one had slipped to the rocks.

With a rush they entered the thicket; but they had not proceeded many yards before they found it almost impassable. Centuries of growth had so interwoven brambles and thorns that it was only by the slow process of stepping over them that an advance could be made, and some of the men had got into places where it was impossible to proceed, and difficult to return.

At length several of them arrived at the

brink of the cliff, and bravely slid to the rocks below. But the whole shore was silent and still. Of course he might be secreting himself behind those huge rocks, and a general search ensued. By this time the greater number of the soldiers had gained the beach, and a systematic pursuit was organized and enforced.

With the full conviction that the prey was near, the troopers hunted with unflagging zeal. Rocks were searched, caves were explored, nothing was untried, but it was a fruitless search.

In the centre of all this turmoil and wasted zeal stood the invisible Lascare.

He heard their suggestions, their passing and repassing, and at last had the gratification to listen to their exclamations of disappointment, and then all sound of the hot pursuit died away.

In a cavern, whose extremity has never yet been explored, hearing their commotion, and within the sound of their voices, stood Lascare. When a boy he had crept through the small aperture, and he now forced his way there a full-grown man. But it was smaller in appearance than in reality, and after the mouth was passed it expanded into a dark but roomy cave, where he stood erect. He took the precaution, after he had passed the mouth, to add again the sand his passing had displaced, that it might seem impossible to give an entrance to a human form.

When the pursuit was over, the three divisions of the troop met at Tregarth, and had again the mortification to return unsuccessful to their barracks, and report a bootless errand.

With slow and cautious step Lascare took the route of the sea side to his home. His knowledge of the locality, and the roaming freaks of his youth, had saved him from the clutch of his pursuers.

CHAPTER XVI.

WHEN night had set in the fugitives cautiously returned, and with timorous step reconnoitred their dwellings before they announced their approach.

As might be conceived, their wives, as well as their neighbours—unconscious what road they had taken—waited their reappearance with anxiety.

That the soldiers had been unsuccessful was evident from their return without a prisoner; and if further evidence was wanting, it was afforded by their moody and dejected appearance; but the satisfaction of the public was incomplete until the harassed and weary men were sheltered under their own roof.

Lascare and Allen sat together that night till a late hour, recounting to each other the events of the day. Companions through life, they had shared together their joys and sorrows, together they had braved the raging sea, when the fierce tempest threatened destruction, and

side by side they had boarded the rich French-
men that an evil fortune had tempted from
their coast. They were now subject to the
same persecutions, and, so far as human fore-
sight could predict, the same fortune would
follow. But the event will show that humanity
can forecast but little of the future. While the
world looks at the external circumstances only,
the internal feelings and dispositions of men
guide to the result.

The two smugglers parted that night in the
mutual hope that all future attempts to seize
them would have a similar termination.

On the following morning the events of the
preceding day were fully discussed by the
people of Tregarth. Many were the conjectures
relating to the place of concealment, in which
no two could agree; and the smugglers wisely
allowed them to settle that matter according to
their own opinion.

But there was one thing that puzzled the
community that was more mysterious. When
the dragoons first visited them, they went
directly, as if by instinct, to the dwelling-
houses of each of the persons they expected to
arrest, which might be accounted for by the
supposition that they had been guided by a

plan of the town ; but on the present occasion they rode through the place with as much speed as the nature of the streets would permit, and passed up the hill at full gallop, until the foaming horses were panting for breath.

How did they discover that the pursued had gone off by that road? How did they know that they were pressing so close to their heels?

" Information " passed from mouth to mouth. Sleek and sly William Meadows mixed with the crowd, in his black cloth suit, shining with use and bygone respectability, and with knowing look, and shaking his head in contempt of such dastardly conduct, whispered, " Information."

Some supposed that the Coast-guard might, by some means unknown, have conveyed the intelligence ; but the appearance of the military was equally a surprise to the officer and his men.

The respectable, unsuspected clerk of Zechariah Drew, banker and miser, still furnished his well-spread board with ill-gotten gains. His evil genius was leading him on to perdition by graduated steps. He began with compunction, proceeded in his course with trembling, advanced to care only for the successful exercise of his ingenuity, and, at length, with treachery, bought gold—gold, even if it should be followed by his victim's blood!

William Meadows alone expected the dragoons, and, when the messenger arrived to warn the smugglers of their approach, he watched their departure. A slip of paper, passing unobserved to the officer before he entered the town, informed him of the course they had taken, and hence the onward pursuit.

While these events were taking place at Tregarth, the affairs of George Millett and Lucy Weston were by no means satisfactory. The Quakers' Quarterly Meeting had passed, and the Annual Meeting—which her father did not attend—and Mr. Weston had made no mention of the subject that he proposed to refer to his friends.

Lucy heard from George through Mrs. Kelly, and they were the happiest moments of her life to be apprised of his welfare; but the uncertain position in which her father had placed her, and its unexpected continuance, was a source of daily grief.

There were times when she had determined to write to George Millett, and tell him that all hope of their union was at an end; and, however painful to her feelings, she would express no regret at the termination—of what? she asked herself. Of an indefinite position of painful uncertainty, she answered. Yet she could write, she thought, that they must cease to regard each other as likely to form any more intimate relationship. She resolved on this from a feeling that by pursuing her present course she was selfishly luring him on in a path that might end in disappointment, that she was inflicting on him gross injustice, wasting his time, and blighting the prospects of a promising life.

"It would be painful," she thought, "to write such a letter; but she could do it, and she would. It was due to George Millett, and it was due to her own consciousness of right."

She sat down at the writing-desk, with the paper before her and the pen in her hand; but she could not write! She made another attempt, but she was too agitated to proceed; and, bursting into tears, slowly closed the desk, with a feeling that she was unequal to the task.

She felt humiliated at her failure. It was the first time in her life she had been

unable to effect the settled purpose of her
mind. But how could she debase herself by
leading George to infer that, after the noble
sacrifice he had made, she was indifferent to
him? Indifferent! When his love was the
solace of a monotonous life!

Perhaps she ought to write, but she could
not do it *now*; and if it must come at *last*, she
would ask him to forgive her, for at present it
was impossible. Poor Lucy Weston was not
equal to the task. Reason and justice bade
her write, but she was not an angel; she was
human, and her heart refused to assent to the
dictates of her mind.

While the poor girl was ruminating over
the sufferings of a hope deferred, news of the
recent escape of Lascare was brought to Penwith, and she resolved on a journey to Tregarth.
There lived one that would feel her sorrow; and
although Edith could afford no help, she would
share her grief. Lucy was also desirous of
seeing Lascare. Edith's description of him
had added to her curiosity; but Edith was
imaginative, and would naturally paint a
favourable portrait of the idol of her heart.
Still he could be no ordinary man, she thought;
for impetuous and confiding as Edith was, she

was also discerning, and keenly alive to anything incongruous.

The first fine day after the arrival of the
news of the futile military pursuit, Lucy proceeded to Tregarth.

She found Edith elated at her husband's
recent escape, and appeared unaffected by the
terrors of the past or fears for the future.
Lucy said nothing to restrain the high spirits
of her friend. There was enough in the world,
she thought, to perform that service, without
any gratuitous assistance; but she had an
inward conviction that her delight was the
precursor of further trouble.

While they were sitting together, discoursing
on the affairs that nearly concerned the interests
of both, Lascare entered, and Edith—proudly,
as Lucy thought,—introduced Richard to her
early friend.

There stood Lascare—the husband of her
foster-sister—a man whose intrepidity had won
a renown that sixty years have not effaced;
whose daring adventures had exasperated the
Government, that had been baffled in every
attempt to secure him. Even now, deterred
by forces he could not withstand, and wishing
to pass his life in the seclusion of his native

hills, he was pursued with unrelenting persecution; but, trusting to the guardianship of
his friends, he dauntlessly paraded the streets
of the remote little town.

He was rather above the ordinary height,
and broad-chested. His figure was sym-
metrical, and his limbs were not large, but
muscular.

He appeared to be a man capable of accom-
plishing a work that required a combination of
strength and agility.

His features were regular, and his expression, in its ordinary mood, was mild and
generous; but his complexion was as dark as
an Andalusian, the blood of which race, in all
probability, swelled his veins. His black,
curling hair, was of glossy brightness, and was
a suitable accompaniment to his dark, piercing
eye; and altogether he presented the appearance of a handsome buccaneer.

His amiable disposition won the regard of
all his neighbours, but he was capable of being
aroused to a fierce achievement when he had
determined on a resolute course. On such
occasions his ordinary aspect disappeared; his
dark eyelashes projected, his eye became fixed,
and his mouth compressed. In this frame,

consequences were disregarded; he would pull
down the pillars of Gaza, though he might be
buried in the ruins.

He possessed the singular faculty of in-
spiring his crew with esteem for his person
and respect for his authority, more from the
innate force of his character than the importance of his command.

> " He swayed their souls with that com-
>   manding art
> That dazzles, leads, yet chills the vulgar
>   heart;
> What is that spell, that thus his lawless
>   train
> Confess and envy, yet oppose in vain?"

His manners were easy and unobtrusive, for
his angularities had been worn off by his intercourse with the world; and his natural rough-
ness had been subdued by the softening
influence of his wife.

This was Edith Phinn's husband, introduced
for the first time to her dearest friend.

At first Lucy did not sufficiently estimate
the character of Lascare, but when his countenance became animated in conversation, and
she observed his quick eye giving expression to

his words, she became aware of his energetic power and unconquerable will. She saw the spell that had fixed the devotion of Edith Phinn.

He was gentle and good, but bold and daring.

There were women in the world, and very good women too, performing the daily avocations of life with scrupulous care and methodical exactitude, to whom Lascare would be repellent; but to a girl of the temperament of Edith Phinn he was dangerously fascinating. There was an affinity of character in those two more binding than the marriage tie.

Lucy congratulated Lascare on his many successful escapes, and Lascare thanked her for the many journeys she had taken on his account.

" I must also ask the favour," said he, " that you will inform Mr. Weston that I feel deeply obliged to him for the assistance he gave me in my correspondence with Edith while I was at Bristol."

" He was very much gratified," said Lucy, " to have it in his power. I am glad you have introduced the subject, or I might have forgotten that my father wishes to be informed how you discovered that your enemies were in pursuit, that he may reply to the inquiries of Samuel Cleave, who is also anxious to know if you are safe."

"It was a gratification that was denied me," said Lascare, "to thank Mr. Cleave in person. I meant to trouble him with my last letter, and to thank him for his kindness; but on leaving his office in the morning, I saw, watching for me at the corner of the street, the satanic countenance of the man whose prying curiosity had caused me apprehension for some days before. I dared not go again to see Mr. Cleave. I went to another part of the city, and waited for an opportunity to escape. I was well disguised, and don't think I should have been discovered; but how it happened that there was no search for me, I can't tell."

"Mr. Cleave explains that," said Lucy. "He kept them in conversation till night, that they might defer their pursuit till the morning."

"That accounts for the absence of all inquiry," said Lascare. "In the morning I was reaching down the Severn with flowing sheet. Mr. Weston will do me another favour, if he will inform Mr. Cleave that I am very grateful for his kindness, which may have saved me from the gallows! I do not fear death, but I dread such an ignominious dangling as that!"

"Richard! You must not talk of it," intruded his impetuous wife, whose cheerfulness had evaporated during the discourse. "I cannot bear the mention of such a subject!"

Lucy, without noticing the interruption, cleverly led off the conversation to another topic, and they were soon talking of events of a more hopeful hue.

They spent the rest of the day pleasantly, and Lucy returned in the evening to Penwith, ruminating over the critical position of her friends, which they appeared to disregard. They felt confident that they should have timely notice of any further pursuit; but the Quakeress was less sanguine; she feared an accident, but her foreboding thoughts lay in concealment.

About a fortnight after this visit a remarkable placard was issued by the Board of Customs, that proved too clearly that they had not abandoned the prosecution. It was to the following effect:—

G. R.

" Notice is hereby given that any person or persons, other than the actual offender, who shall give information at the Custom-house of Penwith which shall lead to the conviction of the murderer of Samuel Williams, late of His Majesty's Coast-guard, who was killed by a shot from the smuggling cruiser, Swift, shall receive two hundred pounds reward and a free pardon."

This startling announcement produced the utmost consternation at Tregarth. Men met in groups to speculate on the consequences that might ensue. They had looked on the affair as a fight, it was now called a murder! Some were persuaded that there would be no informer; others guessed that the temptation might be too much for the three younger men, who had gone to sea; but all were grieved that it had taken so serious and unexpected a turn.

Lascare rendered himself less conspicuous for a few weeks after the publication of this placard; but then, as nothing further was heard of it, he again visited his friends without any suspicion of danger.

But after a while it was remarked, that although Lascare was supposed to be in the most dangerous position, Allen passed the time in greater seclusion. There were whisperings that he was from home, and a feeling of alarm disturbed the people. At length a meeting of the secret committee was convened, and one of their number, with a gravity significant of its importance, produced a written paper. There was no date, no signature, no address; but the hand-writing was known, it was relied on as authentic, and it contained the following words :—

" Edward Allen has given information at the Custom-house that it was Richard Lascare who shot Samuel Williams. An order has been received from head-quarters to spare no expense, and to employ any amount of force that may be required for his apprehension. Allen is under the protection of the Government."

This important missive filled the conclave with dismay.

The men looked at each other in speechless

amazement. John Spillar was the first that rose—for it was he that brought the missive—and placing one hand on the table, and holding the writing in the other, he hesitated a little before he could give expression to his feelings. A fierce spirit of indignation was depicted in his countenance, and when the words came, they were pronounced in slow and measured tones.

"I don't ask you to believe this," said he; "it is too bad to be believed; but I've not seen Ned Allen for a week, and the man that sent this paper never deceived us."

"When did you get the paper?" cried two or three voices at once.

"This morning, from Mr. Drew."

"What is to be done?"

"I wouldn't condemn Ned," said Spillar, "without proof. If he is from home at this moment it is proof enough. But I find it hard to believe. If we find en to be the villain that this paper makes en out to be, nothing in this world would please me so much as to see en hanging at the yard-arm. Let some one inquire if he's home, and, if not, how long he's been away."

One of the smugglers undertook to investigate the matter, and proceeded to Allen's house.

He found his wife and three children at home, and having asked to see Ned, he noticed the alarm that affected the wife. The children, too, gathered around their mother, the two younger ones holding by her apron. They looked up to her countenance, as if to gather the import of the conversation more by the expression that might be evinced than a knowledge of the discourse.

The dread that was depicted on Nancy Allen's features at the sudden mention of her husband's name found a sympathetic reflection in her little ones; and the man was afterwards thankful that they were present, for their helpless innocence prevented an outbreak of the exasperation he felt.

"Is Ned home, Nancy?"

"No, he isn't in the house."

"Was he home last night?"

"No; when he went away he said he mightn't come home for the night."

"When did he go away?"

"Four days ago."

"Was it six days ago he went away?"

"I think it was."

" Did he tell 'ee what business he 'd got in hand ?"

" No."

At this question the tears glistened in her eyes.

" Tell the naughty man to go away," said the little girl. " Go away, naughty man."

" I 'll go away, my little lamb," said the old sailor; and without another word he left the house. He was a husband and a father, and if sorrow and disgrace had come upon the household, he could pity the helpless victims, while he condemned the instrument of their grief.

The smuggler returned to his comrades, and related the substance of the information he had obtained, which confirmed the intelligence conveyed in the secret scrip.

It was now without doubt that Allen had received a free pardon, and would obtain the promised reward should the victim of his treachery be secured.

The first feeling of these faithful associates was a savage desire to wreak their vengeance on the wretch that had betrayed them; their next, to provide for the safety of Lascare. The villainy of the one was contrasted with the generous and confiding disposition of the other; and if at that moment an attack had been made on the person of Lascare it would have been successful only over the dead bodies of this faithful band.

The past lives of the two men were discussed, and if they had selected from their small community two men who would be faithful to each other it would have been Allen and Lascare.

As soon as they were able to handle an oar, Allen and Lascare fished together. They were comrades in the privateer, they were companions in the Swift. They had shared each other's dangers in storm and fight, and had both miraculously escaped the pursuit of the dragoons; but the desire of the one to escape from a harassing persecution, and the cursed thirst for gold, had led him to betray the companion of his youth and the friend of his life.

There was no excuse on account of the necessities of his family, for the smugglers had continued his wages as if he had been in actual employment, and they supplied every means for his protection that could possibly be devised; but all these considerations did not

prevent his exposing his comrade and neighbour to the bitter penalty of death.

The astonishment and exasperation of the
people were excessive, and deep and loud were
the curses that were heaped on the head of the
treacherous informer. The poor wife secluded
herself and her little ones from their bitter
reproaches; who, left alone and exposed to
the wrath of the community, sheltered herself
and innocent children within her closed door.

NOVEMBER, 1875.

SAMUEL TINSLEY'S

PUBLICATIONS.

London:

SAMUEL TINSLEY,

10, SOUTHAMPTON STREET, STRAND.

. *Totally distinct from any other firm of Publishers.*

39

NOTICE.

A WOMAN TO BE WON. An Anglo-Indian
Sketch. By ATHENE BRAMA. 2 vols., 21s.
  " She is a woman, therefore may be wooed ;
  She is a woman, therefore may be won."
                    —TITUS ANDRONICUS, Act ii., Sc. 1.
"A welcome addition to the literature connected with the most pic-
turesque of our dependencies."—*Athenæum.*
"As a tale of adventure " A Woman to be Won" is entitled to decided
commendation."—*Graphic.*
"A more familiar sketch of station life in India . . . . has never been
written. . . . ."—*Nonconformist.*

BARBARA'S WARNING. By the Author of " Recommended to Mercy." 3 vols., 31s. 6d.

BETWEEN TWO LOVES. By ROBERT J. GRIF-
FITHS, LL.D. 3 vols., 31s. 6d.

BLUEBELL. By Mrs. G. C. HUDDLESTON. 3 vols.,
31s. 6d.
"Sparkling, well-written, spirited, and may be read with certainty of
amusement."—*Sunday Times.*

BORN TO BE A LADY. By KATHERINE HEN-
DERSON. Crown 8vo, 7s. 6d.
"Miss Henderson has written a really interesting story. . . . The 'local
colouring' is excellent, and the subordinate characters, Jeanie's father
especially, capital studies."—*Athenæum.*

BRANDON TOWER. A Story. 3 vols., 31s. 6d.
  " Familiar matter of to-day."

BUILDING UPON SAND. By ELIZABETH J.
LYSAGHT. Crown 8vo., 10s. 6d.
"We can safely recommend 'Building upon Sand.'"—*Graphic.*

CHASTE AS ICE, PURE AS SNOW. By Mrs.
M. C. DESPARD. 3 vols., 31s. 6d. Second Edition.
  "A novel of something more than ordinary promise."—*Graphic.*

CINDERELLA : a New Version of an Old Story.
Crown 8vo, 7s. 6d.

CLAUDE HAMBRO. By JOHN C. WESTWOOD. 3
vols., 31s. 6d.

CRUEL CONSTANCY. By KATHARINE KING,
Author of 'The Queen of the Regiment.' 3 vols., 31s. 6d.

DISINTERRED. From the Boke of a Monk of Carden Abbey. By T. ESMONDE. Crown 8vo., 7s. 6d.

DR. MIDDLETON'S DAUGHTER. By the Author of "A Desperate Character." 3 vols., 31s. 6d.

DULCIE. By LOIS LUDLOW. 3 vols., 31s. 6d.

EMERGING FROM THE CHRYSALIS. By J. F. NICHOLLS. Crown 8vo, 7s. 6d.

FAIR, BUT NOT FALSE. By EVELYN CAMPBELL. 3 vols., 31s. 6d.

FAIR, BUT NOT WISE. By Mrs. FORREST-GRANT. 2 vols., 21s.

FIRST AND LAST. By F. VERNON-WHITE. 2 vols., 21s.

FLORENCE; or, Loyal Quand Même. By FRANCES ARMSTRONG. Crown 8vo., 5s., cloth. Post free.
"A very charming love story, eminently pure and lady-like in tone."— *Civil Service Review.*

FAIR IN THE FEARLESS OLD FASHION. By CHARLES FARMLET. 2 vols., 21s.

FOLLATON PRIORY. 2 vols., 21s.

FRIEDEMANN BACH; or, The Fortunes of an Idealist. Adapted from the German of A. E. BRACHVOGEL. By the Rev. J. WALKER, B.C.L. Dedicated, with permission, to H.R.H. the PRINCESS CHRISTIAN of SCHLESWIG-HOLSTEIN. 1 vol., crown 8vo, 7s. 6d.

GAUNT ABBEY. By ELIZABETH J. LYSAGHT, Author of "Building upon Sand," "Nearer and Dearer," etc. 3 vols., 31s. 6d.

GOLD DUST. A Story. 3 vols., 31s. 6d.

GOLDEN MEMORIES. By EFFIE LEIGH. 2 vols., 21s.

GRAYWORTH: a Story of Country Life. By CAREY HAZELWOOD. 3 vols., 31s. 6d.

GRANTHAM SECRETS.   By Phœbe M. Feilden
3 vols.   31s. 6d.

GREED'S LABOUR LOST.   By the Author of
"Recommended to Mercy," etc.   3 vols., 31s. 6d.

HER GOOD NAME.   By J. Fortrey Bouverie.
3 vols., 31s. 6d.

HER IDOL.   By Maxwell Hood.   3 vols., 31s. 6d.

HILDA AND I.   By Mrs. Winchcombe Hartley.
2 vols., 21s.

"An interesting, well-written, and natural story."—*Public Opinion.*

HILLESDEN ON THE MOORS.   By Rosa Mackenzie Kettle, Author of "The Mistress of Langdale
Hall." 2 vols., 21s.

HIS LITTLE COUSIN.   By Emma Maria Pearson,
Author of "One Love in a Life." 3 vols., 31s. 6d.

IN BONDS, BUT FETTERLESS: a Tale of Old
Ulster.   By Richard Cuninghame.   2 vols., 21s.

IN SECRET PLACES.   By Robert J. Griffiths,
LL.D.   3 vols., 31s. 6d.

IN SPITE OF FORTUNE.   By Maurice Gay.   3 vols.,
31s. 6d.

IS IT FOR EVER ?   By Kate Mainwaring.   3 vols.,
31s. 6d.

JOHN   FENN'S   WIFE.   By   Maria   Lewis.
Crown 8vo., 7s. 6d.

KATE BYRNE.   By S. Howard Taylor.   2 vols.,
21s.

KATE RANDAL'S BARGAIN.   By Mrs. Eiloart,
Author of "The Curate's Discipline," "Some of Our
Girls," "Meg," &c.   3 vols., 31s. 6d.

KITTY'S RIVAL. By SYDNEY MOSTYN, Author of 'The Surgeon's Secret,' etc. 3 vols., 31s. 6d.

"Essentially dramatic and absorbing. . . . . We have nothing but unqualified praise for 'Kitty's Rival.'"—*Public Opinion*.

LADY LOUISE. By KATHLEEN ISABELLE CLARGES. 3 vols., 31s. 6d.

LALAGE. By AUGUSTA CHAMBERS. Crown 8vo, 7s. 6d.

LASCARE: a Tale. 3 vols., 31s. 6d.

LEAVES FROM AN OLD PORTFOLIO. By ELIZA MARY BARRON. Crown 8vo, 7s. 6d.

LORD CASTLETON'S WARD. By Mrs. B. R. GREEN. 3 vols., 31s. 6d.

"Mrs. Green has written a novel which will hold the reader entranced from the first page to the last."—*Morning Post*.

MARGARET MORTIMER'S SECOND HUSBAND. By Mrs. HILLS. 1 vol., 7s. 6d.

MARRIED FOR MONEY. 1 vol., 10s. 6d.

"Well written, and full of incident. . . . . . those persons, therefore, who like to be carried on quickly from one event to another, will certainly get what they want in 'Married for Money.'"— *Western Morning News*.

"Characters are sketched with some degree of power, and there is no little ingenuity in the way in which the final catastrophe is contrived.—*Scotsman*.

"Far from ill-written, or uninteresting."—*Graphic*.

MART AND MANSION: a Tale of Struggle and Rest. By PHILIP MASSINGER. 3 vols., 31s. 6d.

MARY GRAINGER: A Story. BY GEORGE LEIGH. 2 vols., 21s.

MR. VAUGHAN'S HEIR. By FRANK LEE BENEDICT, Author of "Miss Dorothy's Charge," etc. 3 vols., 31s. 6d.

MUSICAL TALES, PHANTASMS, AND SKETCHES. From the German of ELISE POLKO. Dedicated (with permission) to Sir Julius Benedict. Crown 8vo, 7s. 6d.

NEARER AND DEARER. By ELIZABETH J. LYSAGHT, Author of "Building upon Sand." 3 vols., 31s. 6d.

NEGLECTED; a Story of Nursery Education Forty Years Ago. By Miss JULIA LUARD. Crown 8vo., 5s. cloth.

NO FATHERLAND. By MADAME VON OPPEN. 2 vols., 21s.

NORTONDALE CASTLE. 1 vol., 7s. 6d.

NOT TO BE BROKEN. By W. A. CHANDLER. Crown 8vo., 10s. 6d.

ONE FOR ANOTHER. By EMMA C. WAIT. Crown 8vo, 7s. 6d.

ONLY SEA AND SKY. By ELIZABETH HINDLEY. 2 vols., 21s.

OVER THE FURZE. By ROSA M. KETTLE, Author of the "Mistress of Langdale Hall," etc. 3 vols., 31s. 6d.

PERCY LOCKHART. By F. W. BAXTER. 2 vols., 21s.

PUTTYPUT'S PROTÉGÉE; or, Road, Rail, and River. A Story in Three Books. By HENRY GEORGE CHURCHILL. Crown 8vo., (uniform with "The Mistress of Langdale Hall"), with 14 illustrations by WALLIS MACKAY. Post free, 4s. Second edition.

"It is a lengthened and diversified farce, full of screaming fun and comic delineation—a reflection of Dickens, Mrs. Malaprop, and Mr. Boucicault, and dealing with various descriptions of social life. We have read and laughed, pooh-poohed, and read again, ashamed of our interest, but our interest has been too strong for our shame. Readers may do worse than surrender themselves to its melo-dramatic enjoyment. From title-page to colophon, only Dominie Sampson's epithet can describe it- it is 'prodigious.'"—*British Quarterly Review*.

RAVENSDALE. By ROBERT THYNNE, Author of "Tom Delany." 3 vols., 31s. 6d.

"A well-told, natural, and wholesome story."—*Standard*.
"No one can deny merit to the writer."—*Saturday Review*.

RUPERT REDMOND: A Tale of England, Ireland, and America. By WALTER SIMS SOUTHWELL. 3 vols., 31s. 6d.

Samuel Tinsley, 10, Southampton Street. Strand.

SAINT SIMON'S NIECE. By FRANK LEE BENEDICT, Author of "Miss Dorothy's Charge." 3 vols., 31s. 6d.

From the **Spectator**, July 24th :—'' A new and powerful novelist has arisen . . . We rejoice to recognise a new novelist of real genius, who knows and depicts powerfully some of the most striking and overmastering passions of the human heart . . . It is seldom that we rise from the perusal of a story with the sense of excitement which Mr. Benedict has produced."

From the **Scotsman**, June 11th :—"Mr. Frank Lee Benedict may not be generally recognised as such, but he is one of the cleverest living novelists of the school of which Miss Braddon was the founder and remains the chief. He is fond of a 'strong' plot, and besprinkles his stories abundantly with startling incidents . . . The story is written with remarkable ability, and its interest is thoroughly well sustained."

SELF-UNITED. By Mrs. HICKES BRYANT. 3 vols., 31s. 6d.

Westminster Review :—"'Self-United' has many marks of no ordinary kind . . . The style is excellent, the conversation bright and natural, the plot good, and the interest well sustained up to the last moment."

SHINGLEBOROUGH SOCIETY. 3 vols., 31s. 6d.

SIR MARMADUKE LORTON. By the Hon. A. S. G. CANNING. 3 vols., 31s. 6d.

SKYWARD AND EARTHWARD : a Tale. By ARTHUR PENRICE. 1 vol., crown 8vo, 7s. 6d.

SPOILT LIVES. By MRS. RAPER. Crown 8vo, 7s. 6d.

SOME OF OUR GIRLS. By Mrs. EILOART, Author of "The Curate's Discipline," "The Love that Lived," "Meg," etc., etc. 3 vols., 31s. 6d.

"A book that should be read."—*Athenæum.*

SONS OF DIVES. 2 vols., 21s.

SQUIRE HARRINGTON'S SECRET. By GEORGE W. GARRETT. 2 vols., 21s.

STANLEY MEREDITH : a Tale. By "SABINA." Crown 8vo, 7s. 6d.

STRANDED, BUT NOT LOST. By DOROTHY BROMYARD. 3 vols., 31s. 6d.

SWEET IDOLATRY. By MISS ANSTRUTHER. Crown 8vo, 7s. 6d.

Samuel Tinsley, 10, Southampton Street, Strand.

THE ADVENTURES OF MICK CALLIGHIN, M.P., a Story of Home Rule ; and THE DE BURGHOS, a Romance. By W. R. ANCKETILL. In one Volume, with Illustrations. Crown 8vo, 7s. 6d.

THE BARONET'S CROSS. By MARY MEEKE, Author of " Marion's Path through Shadow to Sunshine." 2 vols., 21s.

THE BRITISH SUBALTERN. By an Ex-SUBALTERN. 1 vol., 7s. 6d.

THE D'EYNCOURTS OF FAIRLEIGH. By THOMAS ROWLAND SKEMP. 3 vols., 31s. 6d.

THE HEIR OF REDDESMONT. 3 vols., 31s. 6d.

THE INSIDIOUS THIEF: a Tale for Humble Folks. By One of Themselves. Crown 8vo., 5s. Second Edition.

THE LOVE THAT LIVED. By Mrs. EILOART, Author of " The Curate's Discipline," " Just a Woman," " Woman's Wrong," &c. 3 vols., 31s. 6d.

" Three volumes which most people will prefer not to leave till they have read the last page of the third volume."—*Pall Mall Gazette.*

" One of the most thoroughly wholesome novels we have read for some time."—*Scotsman.*

THE MAGIC OF LOVE. By Mrs. FORREST-GRANT, Author of " Fair, but not Wise." 3 vols., 31s. 6d.

" A very amusing novel."—*Scotsman.*

THE MISTRESS OF LANGDALE HALL: a Romance of the West Riding. By ROSA MACKENZIE KETTLE. Complete in one handsome volume, with Frontispiece and Vignette by PERCIVAL SKELTON. 4s., post free.

" The story is interesting and very pleasantly written, and for the sake of both author and publisher we cordially wish it the reception it deserves." —*Saturday Review.*

THE SECRET OF TWO HOUSES. By FANNY FISHER. 2 vols., 21s.

THE SEDGEBOROUGH WORLD. By A. FARE-BROTHER. 2 vols., 21s.

THE SHADOW OF ERKSDALE. By BOURTON MARSHALL. 3 vols, 31s. 6d.

THE SURGEON'S SECRET. By Sydney Mostyn,
Author of " Kitty's Rival," etc. Crown 8vo., 10s. 6d.

"A most exciting novel—the best on our list. It may be fairly recommended as a very extraordinary book."—*John Bull.*

THE THORNTONS OF THORNBURY. By Mrs.
Henry Lowther Chermside. 3 vols., 31s. 6d.

THE TRUE STORY OF HUGH NOBLE'S
FLIGHT. By the Authoress of " What Her Face Said."
10s. 6d.

"A pleasant story, with touches of exquisite pathos, well told by one
who is master of an excellent and sprightly style."—*Standard.*

THE WIDOW UNMASKED; or, the Firebrand in
the Family. By Flora F. Wylde. 3 vols., 31s. 6d.

TIMOTHY CRIPPLE; or, " Life's a Feast." By
Thomas Auriol Robinson. 2 vols., 21s.

"This is a most amusing book, and the author deserves great credit for
the novelty of his design, and the quaint humour with which it is worked
out."—*Public Opinion.*

TIM'S CHARGE. By Amy Campbell. 1 vol., crown
8vo, 7s. 6d.

TOO LIGHTLY BROKEN. 3 vols., 31s. 6d.

"A very pleasing story . . . . . very prettily told."—*Morning Post.*

TOM DELANY. By Robert Thynne, Author of
" Ravensdale." 3 vols., 31s. 6d.

"A very bright, healthy, simply-told story."—*Standard.*

"All the individuals whom the reader meets at the gold-fields are well-
drawn, amongst whom not the least interesting is 'Terrible Mac.'"—*Hour*

"There is not a dull page in the book."—*Scotsman.*

TOWER HALLOWDEANE. 2 vols., 21s.

TOXIE: a Tale. 3 vols., 31s. 6d.

TWIXT CUP and LIP. By Mary Lovett-Cameron.
3 vols., 31s. 6d.

"Displays signs of more than ordinary promise. . . . As a whole the
novel cannot fail to please. Its plot is one that will arrest attention; and
its characters, one and all, are full of life and have that nameless charm
which at once attracts and retains the sympathy of the reader."—*Daily
News.*

'TWIXT WIFE AND FATHERLAND. 2 vols., 21s.

"A bright, vigorous, and healthy story, and decidedly above the average of books of this class. Being in two volumes it commands the reader's unbroken attention to the very end."—*Standard.*

"It is by someone who has caught her (Baroness Tautphoeus') gift of telling a charming story in the boldest manner, and of forcing us to take an interest in her characters, which writers, far better from a literary point of view, can never approach."—*Athenæum.*

TWO STRIDES OF DESTINY. By S. BROOKES BUCKLEE. 3 vols., 31s. 6d.

UNDER PRESSURE. By T. E. PEMBERTON. 2 vols., 21s.

WAGES: a Story in Three Books. 3 vols., 31s. 6d.

WANDERING FIRES. By Mrs. M. C. DESPARD, Author of "Chaste as Ice," &c. 3 vols., 31s. 6d.

WEBS OF LOVE. (I. A Lawyer's Device. II. Sancta Simplicitas.) By G. E. H. 1 vol., Crown 8vo., 10s. 6d.

WEIMAR'S TRUST. By Mrs. EDWARD CHRISTIAN. 3 vols., 31s. 6d.

WHO CAN TELL? By A MERE HAZARD. Crown 8vo, 7s. 6d.

WILL SHE BEAR IT? A Tale of the Weald. 3 vols., 31s. 6d.

"This is a clever story, easily and naturally told, and the reader's interest sustained throughout. . . . A pleasant, readable book, such as we can heartily recommend."—*Spectator.*

WOMAN'S AMBITION. By M. L. LYONS. 1 vol., 7s. 6d.

THIRTIETH THOUSAND.

YE VAMPYRES! A Legend of the National Betting Ring, showing what became of it. By the SPECTRE. In striking Illustrated Cover, price 2s., post free.

Samuel Tinsley, 10, Southampton Street, Strand.

ROBA D'ITALIA; or, Italian Lights and Shadows: a record of Travel. By CHARLES W. HECKETHORN. In 2 vols., 8vo, price 30s.

THE EMPEROR AND THE GALILEAN: an Historical Drama. Translated from the Norwegian of HENRIK IBSEN, by CATHERINE RAY. In 1 vol., crown 8vo, 7s. 6d.

ETYMONIA. In 1 vol., crown 8vo, 7s. 6d.

HOW I SPENT MY TWO YEARS' LEAVE; or, My Impressions of the Mother Country, the Continent of Europe, the United States of America, and Canada. By an Indian Officer. In one vol. 8vo. Handsomely bound. Price 12s.

FACT AGAINST FICTION. The Habits and Treatment of Animals Practically Considered. Hydrophobia and Distemper. With some remarks on Darwin. By the HON. GRANTLEY F. BERKELEY. 2 vols., 8vo., 30s.

MALTA SIXTY YEARS AGO. With a Concise History of the Order of St. John of Jerusalem, the Crusades, and Knights Templars. By Col. CLAUDIUS SHAW. Handsomely bound in cloth, 10s. 6d., gilt edges, 12s.

ON THE MISMANAGEMENT OF THE PUBLIC RECORD OFFICE. By J. PYM YEATMAN, Barrister-at-Law. In Wrapper, price 1s.

LETTER TO THE QUEEN ON HER RETIRE-MENT FROM PUBLIC LIFE. By One of Her Majesty's most Loyal Subjects. In wrapper, price 1s., post free.

THE USE AND ABUSE OF IRRATIONAL ANI-MALS; with some Remarks on the Essential Moral Difference between Genuine "Sport" and the Horrors of Vivisection. In wrapper, price 1s.

CONFESSIONS OF A WEST-END USURER. In Illustrated Cover, price 1s.

THE TICHBORNE AND ORTON AUTOGRAPHS; comprising Autograph Letters of Roger Tichborne, Arthur Orton (to Mary Ann Loder), and the Defendant (early letters to Lady Tichborne, &c.), in facsimile. In wrapper, price 6d.

HARRY'S BIG BOOTS : a Fairy Tale, for "Smalle Folke." By S. E. GAY. With 8 Full-page Illustrations and a Vignette by the author, drawn on wood by PERCIVAL SKELTON. Crown 8vo., handsomely bound in cloth, price 5s.

"Some capital fun will be found in ' Harry's Big Boots.' . . . The illustrations are excellent, and so is the story."—*Pall Mall Gazette.*

MOVING EARS. By the Ven. Archdeacon WEAKHEAD, Rector of Newtown, Kent. 1 vol., crown 8vo., 5s.

A TRUE FLEMISH STORY. By the Author of "The Eve of St. Nicholas." In wrapper, 1s.

THE PHYSIOLOGY OF THE SECTS. Crown 8vo., price 5s.

ANOTHER WORLD; or, Fragments from the Star City of Montalluyah. By HERMES. Third Edition, revised, with additions. Post 8vo., price 12s.

THE FALL OF MAN : An Answer to Mr. Darwin's "Descent of Man ;" being a Complete Refutation, by common-sense arguments, of the Theory of Natural Selection. 1s., sewed.

THE RITUALIST'S PROGRESS; or, A Sketch of the Reforms and Ministrations of the Rev. Septimus Alban, Member of the E.C.U., Vicar of S. Alicia, Sloperton. By A B WILDERED Parishioner. Fcp. 8vo. 2s. 6d. cloth.

MISTRESSES AND MAIDS. By HUBERT CURTIS, Author of " Helen," etc. Price 1d.

EPITAPHIANA; or, the Curiosities of Churchyard Literature : being a Miscellaneous Collection of Epitaphs, with an INTRODUCTION. By W. FAIRLEY. Crown 8vo., cloth, price 5s. Post free.

"Entertaining."—*Pall Mall Gazette.*
"A capital collection."—*Court Circular*
"A very readable volume."—*Daily Review.*
"A most interesting book."—*Leeds Mercury.*
"Interesting and amusing." *Nonconformist.*
"Particularly entertaining."—*Public Opinion.*
"A curious and entertaining volume."—*Oxford Chronicle.*
' 'A very interesting collection."—*Civil Service Gazette.*

TWELVE NATIONAL BALLADS (First Series). Dedicated to Liberals of all classes. By PHILHELOT, of Cambridge ; in ornamental cover, price sixpence, post free.

POEMS AND SONNETS. By H. Greenhough Smith, B.A. Fcap, 8vo, 3s. 6d.

GRANADA, AND OTHER POEMS. By M. Sabiston. Fcp. 8vo., 4s.

THE DEATH OF ÆGEUS, and other Poems. By W. H. A. Emra. Fcp. 8vo., 5s.

HELEN, and other Poems. By Hubert Curtis. Fcp. 8vo., 3s. 6d.

MISPLACED LOVE. A Tale of Love, Sin, Sorrow, and Remorse. 1 vol., crown 8vo., 5s.

THE SOUL SPEAKS, and other Poems. By Francis H. Hemery. In wrapper, 1s.

SUMMER SHADE AND WINTER SUNSHINE: Poems. By Rosa Mackenzie Kettle, Author of "The Mistress of Langdale Hall." New Edition. 2s. 6d., cloth.

THE WITCH of NEMI, and other Poems. By Edward Brennan. Crown 8vo., 10s. 6d.

MARY DESMOND, AND OTHER POEMS. By Nicholas J. Gannon. Fcp. 8vo., 4s., cloth. Second Edition.

THE GOLDEN PATH: a Poem. By Isabella Stuart. 6d., sewed.

THE REDBREAST OF CANTERBURY CATHE- DRAL: Lines from the Latin of Peter du Moulin, some- time a Prebendary of Canterbury. Translated by the Rev. F. B. Wells, M.A., Rector of Woodchurch. Handsomely bound, price 1s.

BALAK AND BALAAM IN EUROPEAN COS- TUME. By the Rev. James Kean, M.A., Assistant to the Incumbent of Markinch, Fife. 6d., sewed.

ANOTHER ROW AT DAME EUROPA'S SCHOOL. Showing how John's Cook made an Irish Stew, and what came of it. 6d., sewed.

UNTRODDEN SPAIN, and her Black Country. Being Sketches of the Life and Character of the Spaniard of the Interior. By HUGH JAMES ROSE, M.A., of Oriel College, Oxford; Chaplain to the English, French, and German Mining Companies of Linaries; and formerly Acting Chaplain to Her Majesty's Forces at Dover Garrison. In 2 vols., 8vo., price 30s.

The Times says—"These volumes form a very pleasing commentary on a land and a people to which Englishmen will always turn with sympathetic interest."

The Saturday Review says—"His title of 'Untrodden Spain' is no misnomer. He leads us into scenes and among classes of Spaniards where few English writers have preceded him. . . . We can only recommend our readers to get it and search for themselves. Those who are most intimately acquainted with Spain will best appreciate its varied excellences."

The Spectator says—"The author's kindliness is as conspicuous as his closeness of observation and fairness of judgment; his sympathy with the people inspires his pen as happily as does his artistic appreciation of the country; and both have combined in the production of a work of striking novelty and sterling value."

The Athenæum says—"We regret that we cannot make further extracts, for 'Untrodden Spain' is by far the best book upon Spanish peasant life that we have ever met with."

The Literary Churchman says—"Seldom has a book of travel come before us which has so taken our fancy in reading, and left behind it, when the reading was over, so distinct an impression."

OVER THE BORDERS OF CHRISTENDOM AND ESLAMIAH; or, Travels in the Summer of 1875 through Hungary, Slavonia, Bosnia, Servia, Herzegovina, Dalmatia, and Montenegro to the North of Albania. By JAMES CREAGH, Author of "A Scamper to Sebastopol." 2 vols., large post 8vo, 25s.

ITALY REVISITED. By A. GALLENGA (of *The Times*), Author of "Country Life in Piedmont," &c., &c. 2 vols., 8vo., price 30s.

CANTON AND THE BOGUE: the Narrative of an Eventful Six Months in China. By WALTER WILLIAM MUNDY. Crown 8vo, 7s. 6d.

DICKENS'S LONDON: or, London in the Works of Charles Dickens. By T. EDGAR PEMBERTON, Author of "Under Pressure." Crown 8vo, 6s.

Samuel Tinsley, 10, Southampton Street, Strand.